The Curious Cases of
Cyriack Skinner Grey

Other book collections by Arthur Porges:

Three Porges Parodies and a Pastiche (1988)
The Mirror and Other Strange Reflections (2002)
Eight Problems in Space: The Ensign De Ruyter Stories (2008)
The Adventures of Stately Homes and Sherman Horn (2008)
The Calabash of Coral Island and Other Early Stories (2008)
The Miracle of the Bread and Other Stories (2008)
Spring, 1836: Selected Poems (2008)
The Devil and Simon Flagg and Other Fantastic Tales (2009)

Forthcoming titles by Arthur Porges:

The Ruum and Other Science Fiction Stories
The Rescuer and Other Science Fiction Stories
Collected Essays: Volume One
Collected Essays: Volume Two

The Curious Cases of
Cyriack Skinner Grey

Arthur Porges

Edited by Richard Simms

Richard Simms Publications

This paperback first edition published in 2009

Richard Simms Publications, Surrey, England

ISBN: 978-0-9556942-4-0

With special thanks to Sue Wakefield, Cele Porges and Joel Hoffman.

For more information please visit The Arthur Porges Fan Site:

http://arthurporges.atwebpages.com

Contents

	page
Introduction	9
The Scientist and the Bagful of Water	21
The Scientist and the Wife Killer	29
The Scientist and the Vanished Weapon	39
The Scientist and the Obscene Crime	46
The Scientist and the Multiple Murder	52
The Scientist and the Invisible Safe	66
The Scientist and the Two Thieves	72
The Scientist and the Time Bomb	79
The Scientist and the Platinum Chain	87
The Scientist and the Exterminator	93
The Scientist and the Missing Pistol	101
The Scientist and the Stolen Rembrandt	108
The Scientist and the Impassable Gulf	115
The Scientist and the Poisoner	125
The Scientist and the Heavenly Alibi	136
The Scientist and the One-Word Clue	141
Checklist of Sources	145
About the Author	146

Introduction

Over the course of a long career as a short story writer, Arthur Porges produced a remarkable number of stories concerning crimes of one type or another. The many tales of murder and detection that he wrote outnumber even his numerous fantasy and science fiction stories. For the most part, these appeared in a variety of periodicals wholly devoted to publishing mystery and detective short fiction. Arthur's prolific output in this demanding literary field found a home in such titles as *Mike Shayne Mystery Magazine*, *The Saint Mystery Magazine*, *The Man From U.N.C.L.E. Magazine* and *Offbeat Detective Story Magazine*. Subsequent reprints in numerous anthologies meant that several of the best of these were preserved in book form—though not nearly enough, in this writer's opinion.

The main forums for his mystery short stories were the enduring twin publications *Ellery Queen's Mystery Magazine* and *Alfred Hitchcock's Mystery Magazine*, both still going strong today. (From hereafter I will refer to them as EQMM and AHMM, respectively.) A typical back issue—dating from the 1960s—of either of these two venerable titles would often feature an Arthur Porges story alongside contributions by the likes of Talmage Powell, Ed Lacy, Edward D. Hoch, Jack Ritchie, Frank Sisk, Helen Nielsen and Henry Slesar.

It was to the editors of AHMM and EQMM that Porges sold the majority of his much-loved "locked room" mysteries. Porges excelled in this sub-genre of detective fiction. In these stories a crime, usually a murder, is committed under apparently impossible circumstances. The name "locked room" takes its title from the classic type of mystery story wherein a dead body is found in a locked room with no other entrances.

Arthur's unique contributions to this area are highly regarded among detective short story buffs. In his reference book *Locked Room Murders and Other Impossible Crimes* (Ferret Fantasy Ltd, 1979), Bob Adey, a noted authority on "impossible crime" tales, acknowledges Porges' importance to the field by praising the wealth and originality of his ideas. And Mike Grost, in his superb *A Guide to Classic Mystery and Detection* website, asserts that after John Dickson Carr and Edward D. Hoch, "Porges is the third most productive writer of 'impossible crime' stories."

One has to go back to the 19th and early 20th century to find Porges' literary antecedents. There were of course countless early practitioners of "fair play" detective fiction, where the author provides certain clues within the story to challenge the reader to solve the puzzle before all is explained at the dénouement. Sir Arthur Conan Doyle, R. Austin Freeman, G. K. Chesterton, Agatha Christie, Edgar Allan Poe, John Dickson Carr and Jacques Futrelle, to name just a few—Porges read them all. As a young man he was a voracious reader of classic Golden Age detective novels and short stories.

But for all that, Porges' ideas—as I have remarked in previous introductions—did not only come from his love of fiction. In his letters to me he was apt to stress that inspiration came from his remarkably diverse reading in many different subjects. Through this he would furnish his mind with little known facts, more often than not scientific in nature, which would later provide him with ideas for ingenious plots. It is these ideas that underpin and form the basis of all his "locked room" mysteries.

Like his contemporary Edward D. Hoch, now sadly no longer with us, Porges very much specialized in stories of this type. While a number of these were one-off yarns, Porges created several logicians and sleuths, each of whom appeared in more than one story. Their common trait was an uncanny ability to put their scientific knowledge to effective use in helping the police with difficult-to-solve crimes. "The Big Four," as I like to call them, who featured in dozens of stories, were Joel Hoffman, Julian Morse Trowbridge, Ulysses Price Middlebie and Cyriack Skinner Grey. The latter was the most prolific; in total thirteen Grey stories were published in EQMM, AHMM and *Mike Shayne Mystery Magazine* while a further three went unsold—more on that later.

And so we come to the stories in this collection.

"The Scientist and the Bagful of Water," the opening instalment in a new series of detective stories featuring Cyriack Skinner Grey, appeared in the November 1965 issue of EQMM. Billed by the legendary editor and author Frederic Dannay (one half of Ellery Queen) as a "modern scientific detective," Grey has the distinction of being EQMM's first wheelchair-bound sleuth. The first appearance of Grey also predates the feature-length pilot episode of the NBC television series *Ironside* by a couple of years!

In "The Scientist and the Bagful of Water," the reader is introduced to Cyriack Skinner Grey, a widower and former research scientist who is confined to a wheelchair for life as the result of a mountaineering accident some years earlier. We also make the acquaintance of his 14-year-old son Edgar Grey, who possesses an I.Q. of 180 and acts as his immobilized father's "legs." Completing the triumvirate is Lieutenant Trask, an ex-pupil of Grey's and now a competent and efficient police detective with an unfortunate knack for encountering acutely perplexing cases.

The opening story, which naturally opens this collection, is built on a framework that is repeated throughout the series. The formula is simple and effective, providing a perfect setting for the author's ideas. Lieutenant Trask is investigating a crime, usually a murder or a theft—there are a couple of exceptions to this that I will mention later—when he runs up against an impasse in his routine investigations. Some aspect of the crime, relating to the precise method of the murder itself, or a missing item of vital evidence—a weapon or stolen object—just doesn't add up. The conventional, time-honored investigative procedures are not enough—a less orthodox mental approach to the problem is required.

Given the fact that Cyriack Skinner Grey is now acting as a crime consultant in his retirement, Trask, in every one of these stories, is compelled to call on his old friend at his home and request Grey's help in solving each puzzle. It is these problems that form the bare bones of Porges' ingenious plots. The veritable wealth of cleverly conceived mysteries on display here is what these tales are all about.

"The Scientist and the Bagful of Water," sets the pattern for the whole series. In this particular story, and several others, Trask is confident of a suspect's guilt, but without knowing just *how* the crime was executed, he will not have enough evidence to secure a conviction. Knowing the *modus operandi* is, more often than not, crucial to the successful unraveling of the mystery. One cannot provide an excess of specific information concerning the actual mechanics of each story device, or inventive gimmick, without giving too much away. But a description of a select few of the plots will hopefully give the interested reader (those of you who read the introduction first—no matter if you didn't!) an idea of what to expect.

In this story Lieutenant Trask strongly suspects a business executive of murdering his partner. The victim is killed outright after being hit on the head by a bag of water, weighing over two hundred pounds, which was apparently dropped from a window very high up in an adjacent building. The problem is, the suspect cannot be placed in the building, having actually been close behind his unfortunate partner at the time of the "accident." There is clear evidence that the object that killed the man was indeed a bag containing water. But there is also an obvious motive for the deceased to have been murdered by his partner—the latter stands to inherit millions in the event of his colleague's death. The question presented to Cyriack Skinner Grey is this: how on earth could Trask's number-one-suspect possibly have committed the crime?

To achieve an understanding of the process by which Grey is able to solve the seemingly unsolvable, it is necessary here to attempt a description of his mental processes. First of all, as in this first entry in the series, and subsequent cases, the wheelchair-bound criminologist requires his completely stumped visitor to give him all the facts of the case. As Grey asserts on more than once occasion, "I cannot work without data."

Only then, armed with such information, the police reports, multi-angle photographs, and sundry other salient facts—some not immediately obvious as being pertinent to either Trask or the reader!—relating to the case in question, can the scientist engage in some lateral thinking. For Grey is an intuitive genius, his creative flair augmented by a learned mind; a "storehouse" of scientific knowledge at his disposal. Grey deals in "plausible inferences," and when Trask leaves him to mull over the mystery, he closes his eyes and activates what he calls his "Theater of the Mind." This curious method of visualizing a crime scene enables him to extrapolate from the given data and make educated guesses where others would fail. Exercising practical, applied logic, and utilizing not only his grounding in science (and various byways of specialized knowledge), but also his brilliant imagination, Grey is able to unravel a series of baffling mysteries. His thought processes, I might add, are not always centered on a scientific fact. In more than one of the stories in this book, the key to the problem is actually a matter of logistics, or an inventive manipulation of the physical world on the part of a cunning lawbreaker, in order to hide evidence and baffle the police investigation. Whatever the *modus operandi*, when finally this super-sleuth's unrivalled deductive abilities unlock the solution to the mystery, one can only marvel at Porges' imagination in coming up with such remarkably original plots. Arthur obviously shared Grey's love of a good mystery and the mental challenge it represents.

A spirit of creativity, of "thinking outside the box," is at the heart of the Cyriack Skinner Grey stories. When the scientist tells Trask that science is not a dry area of human endeavor concerned only with marshalling facts and figures, this is surely the author talking. When Arthur, through his character, states that a great deal of imagination is involved in developing theories and devising meaningful experiments, one can perhaps begin to appreciate what truly inspired these tales.

Porges was an enthusiastic defender of science, particularly in his later years, when he noticed that much of modern western society had become increasingly disenchanted with what the scientific world had to offer. His letters to local newspapers, often deploring the rise in Creationism (Porges greatly admired Darwin) testify to this.

Before I go on to focus on several of the later stories in the series, some further background may be worth noting. Earlier on in this essay I commented on those authors whose crime fiction most inspired Arthur's own efforts in the same field. With particular regard to the Grey stories, the two most obvious influences, in terms of format, style and his sleuth's method of solving crimes are, without doubt, those famous past masters of the "impossible crime" sub-genre, John Dickson Carr and Sir Arthur Conan Doyle.

When an exasperated Lieutenant Trask presents Grey with an unusual new case, we are in Sherlock Holmes territory. Trask is Porges' Lestrade. With their ingenuity, scientific detection and devilishly clever plots, the Grey mysteries have as their ancestors the works of both Carr and Doyle. (By the way, these two literary giants have been name-checked in many a Porges story down the years.)

It would not, however, be fair to give the impression that Arthur created the Grey series solely as a tribute to two of his literary heroes. (For Porges' true homage to Doyle, check out the collection of Sherlockian parodies, *The Adventures of Stately Homes and Sherman Horn*, published by The Battered Silicon Dispatch Box in 2008.) Porges' ideas, deftly translated into workable plots, were all his own. It is this aspect that drives the Grey stories and provides the necessary variation: in this book you'll encounter one ingenious plot after another!

The series continued to be published in EQMM in the late 1960s. In these painstakingly crafted stories we follow Grey's examinations of a variety of unusual crimes. One highlight is "The Scientist and the Wife Killer" (1966), where the mystery surrounds the death, by electrocution, of a woman taking a bath. The police think the husband has murdered her, given his track record—he is suspected of killing his two previous spouses for their insurance money—but until now he has escaped justice due to a lack of tangible evidence. The question of just how he achieved this last murderous feat, with no electrical appliances in the bathroom and his being away from the marital home at the time of his wife's death, has Trask knocking on Grey's door.

In this story we witness for the first time the marvelous gadgets of Cyriack Skinner Grey's state-of-the-art wheelchair. By manipulating several controls, the scientist is able to offer his visitor, from various hidden compartments in the arm of the chair, cigars, coffee, lemonade and occasionally something stronger.

We also see more of Edgar, a genius in his own right who plays an important role in securing the evidence required to disprove the serial wife killer's belief that he has pulled off yet another "perfect crime." Edgar possesses the mobility that his father lacks, and performs some of the necessary legwork. Through the gathering of data by intelligent observation, Edgar enables Grey to visit the scene of the crime by proxy.

In this story, and later instalments, there is plenty of banter and good-natured ribbing between Edgar and Lieutenant Trask. These jocular exchanges (Porges had a good ear for dialogue), in addition to the refreshment breaks provided, courtesy of Grey's gadget-laden wheelchair, serve as an effective counterpoint to the otherwise orderly progression of the narrative; the uncompromising element concerned purely with good old-fashioned, no-nonsense problem-solving. This lightening of tone adds color and enjoyment to these stories.

A somewhat unusual entry in the canon is "The Scientist and the Obscene Crime" (1966), which deviates from the standard "howdunit" formula of the series. A twisted pervert is harassing a young woman by bombarding her with a string of lewd phone calls. As conventional methods of tracing the calls have failed, Grey is called upon by Trask to try and devise some way of catching the elusive caller in the act.

Of the first wave of Grey stories, my personal favorite has to be "The Scientist and the Multiple Murder" (1967). This is possibly the most accomplished story in the entire series; it also happens to be the longest. The story's eye-catching premise commands your attention. The scene of the crime is a swimming pool on top of an office building twenty-six stories high. Floating in the water of the pool are the corpses of no less than eight men, all directors of a large corporation. The unfortunate victims appear to have been fatally electrocuted.

The mystery is profound. Trask is faced with the fact that several witnesses who were in the building at the time—though none of them were present on the roof when the eight men died—state categorically there was no way any potential murderer could have gained access to the roof. The nearest buildings are too far away. The quandary is just how the murder could have been achieved. If Trask—with Grey's essential help—can discover the method, he'll find the killer; it soon transpires there are several people with an obvious motive. The solution to this puzzle, in the face of an apparently total lack of clues, is both inventive and unexpected.

The run of stories in EQMM came to an abrupt end with the appearance of the clever "The Scientist and the Invisible Safe" in the May 1967 issue of EQMM. Seven years were to pass before the next Cyriack Skinner Grey story was published. Porges was too busy writing other stories for this to be attributable to any creative inertia, though admittedly his overall fiction output diminished somewhat in the early 1970s.

Grey returned to the mystery short story scene when Arthur started selling a new batch of stories to AHMM, sometimes referred to as EQMM's kid brother (they share the same publisher). Arthur's stories had been appearing in AHMM since 1959.

"The Scientist and the Two Thieves," in the June 1974 issue of AHMM, saw a welcome return for Cyriack Skinner, Edgar Grey and Lieutenant Trask. Picking up where they left off, the endearing trio wastes no time in getting straight into another investigation of a perplexing crime. Still succeeding in solving the unsolvable, Grey's masterful powers of deduction give Trask the solution to the mystery of the inexplicably missing jewelry.

If you have already read several of the stories in this volume you will no doubt have noticed that a sprinkling of literary and historical references enrich these tales. Porges never lets such allusions get in the way of the art of good storytelling. In "The Scientist and the Two Thieves," however, a mention of *The Ingoldsby Legends* leads Grey to a certain clue, which in turn inspires him to an unlikely solution—I for one would never have guessed it!

A true oddity in the series is "The Scientist and the Time Bomb" (1974). Trask shows Grey a most extraordinary letter, written by a man who has been dead for fifteen years. Having instructed his lawyers not to mail the letter until fifteen years after his death, Horace Coleman informs the local authorities that within a few months, the house that had been in his family for generations will be blown up. Not only that, but he refuses to reveal the method by which this will be achieved, stating that nothing can be done to prevent the explosion.

A bomb with a fifteen-year fuse just doesn't seem possible. As bemused as his friend Lieutenant Trask, Grey looks first at the motive. Coleman is (was) profoundly unhappy at the way his ancestral home, a historic mansion now publicly owned, is about to be sold to a private company against his grandfather's express wishes. The letter is primarily intended as a warning, in order to save lives.

Grey then approaches the case from a different angle, believing that if he looks deeply into Coleman's personal background, the nature and location of the hidden device that will cause the destruction of the house might just be ascertained. This story has a fantastic conclusion that, however unlikely, boasts an unassailable logic. These tales are almost too clever by half!

After "The Scientist and the Missing Pistol" (1975), one of two entries in the series to appear in the fondly remembered *Mike Shayne Mystery Magazine*, the final Cyriack Skinner Grey story to be published in AHMM was "The Scientist and the Stolen Rembrandt," which was printed in the February 1975 issue. In this story Trask describes to Grey the peculiar circumstances which led to the disappearance of a newly-discovered drawing by Rembrandt. A "top fence" acquires the valuable sketch and makes off with his illicit acquisition in a fast boat, heading out to sea for a meeting with a prospective buyer. Acting on a tip-off, Trask and the U.S. Coast Guard give chase and eventually manage to board the vessel. The fence, Max Rudolph, is captured, but of the Rembrandt, there is no sign. The challenge that Grey relishes with his usual dedication and aplomb is to locate the hiding place. Hint: there is a reference in this story to Poe's famous story "The Purloined Letter." So what's an obvious hiding place for a drawing on a boat? Or, as Holmes would say, "When you have eliminated the impossible, whatever remains, however unlikely, must be the truth."

Later the same year, the brilliantly realized "The Scientist and the Impassable Gulf" appeared in the October 1975 issue of *Mike Shayne Mystery Magazine*. Even Grey's creative mind and deductive abilities are stretched to the limit in this particularly hard to solve murder case, brought to him as ever by Lieutenant Trask. A woman's strangled body is found in an area of marshland, and the police have their eye on a likely suspect—Jennings Bryan Latimer, who is hilariously named after a noted pacifist (it was typical of Porges' dry humor to throw in a joke like that!). Latimer is a henpecked husband whose bitter, undersexed and acid tongued wife would appear to have pushed him too far. But proving his guilt seems impossible. How did his spouse's corpse get there? The surrounding area reveals no sign of footprints or tracks made either by the victim or the murderer. The woman's dead body seems to have appeared in the marsh out of thin air.

This ended the second run of published stories featuring the ingenious scientist. Note the word "published," as among the batch of stories Arthur intended for the mystery magazine market in the 1970s was "The Scientist and the Poisoner," which went unsold. Just why editors rejected it at the time is something of a puzzle, one that even Grey himself would have had trouble solving! Given the quality of this story, I can offer no explanation, other than to mentally shrug and attribute it to editorial inscrutability. Putting that aside, I am very pleased to publish it here for the first time. Written in 1973, "The Scientist and the Poisoner" has all the strengths of the other stories and, in my opinion, it is one of the best in the entire series.

The story revolves around the murder of a wealthy old gentleman who is poisoned while seated at his usual dinner table in a hotel restaurant. Once again, how the crime was committed is all-important. At first glance, the agency by which the poison reaches the victim is not at all apparent. While the murder method turns out to be typically unusual, and Grey's intuitive genius is as ever a source of wonderment, this entry in the Grey series is marked by a certain poignancy. Hector MacNeil Burrington, although a multi-millionaire, is a kindly old guy, undeserving of his fate. The perpetrators of the crime are pure evil, as Trask angrily reflects. On one level, I found this a strangely moving story.

Porges didn't manage to sell any more of his stories of Cyriack Skinner Grey but, in the ensuing years, he was inspired to bring his scientific sleuth out of retirement for two last cases.

Unpublished until now, "The Scientist and the Heavenly Alibi" is an excellent yarn. It has all the strengths of the earlier stories and includes a most ingenious gimmick concerning the supposed whereabouts of a murder suspect. If he wasn't where he claims to have been, Trask can secure a conviction. As is often the case in these tales, Grey faces a race against time to break a criminal's alibi. Trask is convinced of his suspect's guilt. In this story, he firmly believes the co-owner of a lucrative cattle ranch is guilty of the cold-blooded murder of his partner. But without Grey's essential input, his alibi will protect him from the law. There is a clue in the title of this fascinating, beautifully structured story.

"The Scientist and the One-Word Clue" is a neat little story to close off this collection. Detailing Grey and Trask's search for a clue to the location of some vital, damning evidence on top-level corruption left behind by a murdered investigative reporter, it doesn't quite match the brilliance of the previous story but is still a worthy and intriguing addition to the Grey series.

I feel I cannot end this introduction without commenting on a certain odd fact. "The Scientist and the Heavenly Alibi" and "The Scientist and the One-Word Clue" are marked by a certain inconsistency with the rest of the series. Contrary to my expectations when I first discovered the original manuscripts, Grey's resourceful son Edgar is entirely absent; he doesn't even get an offstage mention. Whether or not this was an oversight on the author's part is open to conjecture.

It doesn't really matter. As these final two stories were penned some years later, one might picture Edgar as being all grown up now, no doubt pursuing a successful career in whatever profession he chose for himself.

In a way, the Cyriack Skinner Grey series never did reach any definite conclusion, so we can happily imagine that Grey, along with Edgar and Trask, is still out there somewhere, sipping his favorite

Kona coffee and solving impossible crimes and "locked room" mysteries in some alternative literary universe …

Richard Simms
Surrey, England
November, 2009

The Scientist and the Bagful of Water

"A little bag of water," Lieutenant Trask said in a troubled voice, "and a man's dead. It's pretty far-fetched, if you ask me, and awfully damned convenient for Preston Forbes Whitney, Junior." He almost spat the last word.

Cyriack Skinner Grey, very erect in his wheelchair, which glittered with several dozen mechanical and electrical gadgets of his own invention, snapped, "How little?" Like Lord Kelvin, Grey was a firm believer in exact measurement. "Water's heavy, and almost incompressible, remember."

If there was a hint of pomposity in his statement, it was only natural, because before becoming a freelance crime consultant, Grey— a brilliant research scientist—had also taught graduate courses in physics. Then a bad fall while mountain climbing had damaged his spinal cord, putting him in a wheelchair for the rest of his life.

Thanks to a number of valuable patents, Grey had no financial problems. He had promptly converted his old rambling house into a huge laboratory, with ramps instead of stairs, and enough expensive equipment to satisfy a university. His only assistant was his 14-year-old son, Edgar; Grey's wife had died some years before.

"I checked with an unbroken bag of the same size," Lieutenant Trask said, feeling a small glow of pleasure as Grey nodded approval. He had once been the scientist's pupil, courtesy of the Police Academy, and knew the worth of Grey's approval. "It will hold about two pounds of water."

"Then it's a simple matter to settle," the scientist said, reaching for the 20-inch slide rule resting in brackets on the side of his wheelchair. But he stopped his motion halfway, and said, "Hell, it's just a little mental arithmetic; I don't need this. What floor of the hotel was the bag dropped from?"

"The convention occupied the nineteenth, but some of those jokers could have operated from other places—corridor windows or fire escapes—above or below that level. Naturally, nobody will admit ever hearing of such tricks—not a practical joker in the crowd!—now that a man's dead."

"We'll assume nineteen, then—say, a hundred and sixty feet. Time of fall, about three seconds: one sixty over sixteen is the square of the time, remember. So velocity at ground, ninety-six feet per second. Energy of hitting man—one half mass times square of velocity—hum—two hundred and eighty-eight foot-pounds." He gave Trask a quizzical glance. "Your victim was hit, so to speak, by a weight of over two hundred pounds falling one foot; or to make it more understandable, say, twenty pounds dropping ten feet. Certainly enough to kill a man."

"Oh, it's reasonable enough," the lieutenant admitted gloomily. "But too convenient for his partner—this Whitney, Junior I mentioned."

"Where does he come in?"

"He comes into a fortune, I'm afraid."

"Just how?"

"He was James Connors' partner in the business, which is worth quite a few millions. Not that he contributed much; but his father was an old friend of Connors', and bought the boy a share some years back. Junior was never any good; now he's a tubby playboy, about as much use to the firm as a price war.

"Anyhow, he and Connors argued and fought a good deal; Whitney was always trying for some angle to increase his take—gambling, foreign cars, and fast women kept him broke. The older man wasn't buying that; the business needed every penny for expansion; the future could be really big if the firm wasn't milked dry. He'd've liked to buy Junior out, but couldn't make it now—not if his ten-year plan was to work out.

"Well, Connors often took a short cut to the parking lot by going through an alley behind the Regency Hotel. That night, Whitney was along. There was this convention—the WOWS—World-Wide Organization of Wolverines, a benevolent association with the usual hard core of swag-bellied, retread delinquents. They'd been dropping bags of water from the upper floors. We warned them it could be dangerous, and the leaders promised to keep the members in line; but you know how it is. Nobody can really control some of those old clowns when they're full of liquor."

"And one of the bags struck and killed Connors?"

"That's what Junior says. He claims they were going through the alley when he hears something come down with a swish; then there was a smacking sound, Connors staggered, grabbed his head with both hands, and collapsed. Whitney yelled for help, and in a few minutes quite a crowd gathered. When one of our cruisers came, Connors was dead, his head and shoulders soaked—no blood, more like a sandbagging—also his jacket; and there was this torn, wet, empty bag on the blacktop."

"Hmmph!" Grey snorted. "Seems pretty convincing, doesn't it?"

"It would—if Junior planned it that way. Suppose he read about the hi-jinks—the WOWS are in town for a week, you know—and deliberately prepared for a kill. He could have clubbed Connors, and set the stage easily enough."

"He'd need some water to pour over the body."

"He could bring that in a flask. It was a chilly night, and Junior wore a topcoat. Connors was pretty warm-blooded, and didn't wear a coat. Maybe Whitney took his to conceal the flask and whatever he used for a club. Wish I'd searched him on the spot, but we just took his statement and let him go; it seemed pretty clear-cut, then.

"I didn't know," Trask added grimly, "what his status in the firm was. For that matter, he would have had plenty of time, before anybody showed up in answer to his yells, to get rid of all the evidence. You can carry water in one of those plastic fish bags that the pet stores use; it crumples up to the size of a peanut when empty."

"What about the club?"

"Hell, anything would do. A fist-sized stone, wrapped in a corner of his coat, so as not to break his skin and draw blood. Then he could simply toss the stone away, and nobody could ever prove it had been used. Or a sockful of dirt. Empty it, and toss the sock a dozen yards away in one of the hotel trash cans."

"All you have, really," Grey pointed out in a dry voice, "is a hypothesis based largely on dislike and suspicion of this Whitney, Junior. It could be true—but so could the innocent, obvious theory of a stupid conventioneer. I don't see where I come in."

"I don't either—I was just hoping," the lieutenant admitted. "I almost had him, I thought, for a while there. I learned that the Regency Hotel had purposely turned off all the water on the convention floor early that evening—trying to teach the visiting firemen a lesson."

"Well?"

"You can't stop a practical joker that easily," Trask said. "There were the toilet flushboxes, and a few full pitchers left. The hotel soon gave it up as hopeless, and turned the water back on. That was after Connors got killed."

The scientist was silent for a moment, his black, almost lusterless eyes hooded. Then he said, "The autopsy showed a fractured skull, I suppose."

"Right. Doc Perkins says a bag of water could have done it. But he admits that so could a lot of other things."

"His hair and jacket were wet, you say?"

"Yes."

"Blacktop, too?"

"Yes, but not much. After all, it was only a small bag of water. But enough to make the point. Junior didn't goof there. A dry blacktop, and I'd've had him cold. I'll bet my seniority he spilled water over Connors, over the blacktop, even on the torn bag, before calling out for help."

"Maybe," Grey said. "But you've no proof—not a scrap."

"I guess it's hopeless," the lieutenant said, getting up to go. "I had a hunch it would be. The easiest way to kill anybody, as every cop knows, is to stage a convincing 'accident.' There may be oodles of suspicion, but in simple situations a jury's always reluctant to assume criminal intent. And when a car's involved," he added wryly, "each juror figures—how rightly!—that he may kill somebody one day himself, and wouldn't want to be considered a murderer just for being drunk and doing a measly fifteen miles an hour over the legal limit."

"True," Grey said. "If I wanted to kill somebody, I'd 'accidentally' back over him on a driveway, or drop a brick from the roof while fixing the chimney, or stumble against the ladder he was on. Nothing to it.

"However, let's not throw in the towel yet. Let me think about it for another day or two. It didn't seem possible for Pasteur to hit on a way to isolate one miserable little bacterium from fifty thousand other kinds, all in the same drop, but it turned out to be very simple—once he thought of smearing a culture plate, and allowing each species to begin a new colony. Merely a matter of dilution."

Grey dexterously wheeled his chair to the door, disdaining the use of the electric motor—rechargeable, of course—in the base. "If I come up with anything remotely helpful, I'll call you. But better not hold your breath," he added, wooden-faced.

Ordinarily, Lieutenant Trask never left Grey without feeling a distinct surge of hope. The scientist had a genius for breaking difficult cases, and he enjoyed the mental exercise, which was not so different from his normal brainwork but had a human element to add spice. It was ostensibly a matter of logic and scientific method; but actually it was nearer poetry, because imagination played so large a role.

The basic concept had to come first—the identification with the criminal and his gimmick—then the application of laboratory science to verification, and—as both men hoped—proof suitable for non-technical jurors. On the other hand, it was Grey's extensive background in all branches of organized knowledge that made his "hunches" fruitful.

But in this case Trask felt no lift of hope. He was asking the impossible, and he knew it. What had happened in that dimly lit alley could never be known for certain. Only an eyewitness could disprove Whitney's account, and there was no witness. The area had been deserted. Even if one of the convention guests had been looking down, there was nothing significant he could have seen in the dark alley from so many floors up. To have spotted the murder, an observer would have had to be within a few feet of the two men; and Junior had made mighty sure nobody was that close when he struck.

Keep it simple—a plausible accident—that was the secret of a successful murder. Those were the kind that went undetected year after year. You didn't find them in the statistics; only the stupid and impulsive killers ever get caught, Trask thought unhappily. No, Preston Forbes Whitney, Junior, would soon control—and probably ruin—a multimillion-dollar business, and was beyond the reach of the law.

Some policemen would have shrugged all this off; win a few; lose a lot. But Lieutenant Trask was a dedicated man, and he hated killers; or, to be more fair to him, he hated killing; for there were murderers he could understand, feel sorry for, and not hate at all. Junior was not so privileged; the crime was too cold-blooded; the victim had been a nice guy.

One day went by, and the lieutenant tried to lose himself in the details of a new case, but his heart was still in the old one, hopeless as it seemed.

Then Grey phoned. The scientist came gruffly to the point.

"Still got Connors' jacket?" he barked.

"His jacket?" Trask was bewildered for a moment. "I guess we have. There was no reason to rush it back to the heirs."

"Heirs?" Grey sounded indignant; he hated being deprived of possibly relevant facts. "But I thought Whitney—"

"He gets control of the business—and that was a damned silly arrangement: an invitation for him to murder Connors. But there are plenty of other assets for sisters, cousins, and aunts. Plus what they can salvage of the firm before Junior bleeds it to death."

"I see. Not that it's relevant. But if you have the jacket, I'll send Edgar over for it."

"Certainly. But what good—?"

"I'll explain that later—if the notion pays off. Been talking to the Maintenance Chief at the Regency; very intelligent chap, by the way. We may have a chance, after all. Edgar'll be right over." And Grey hung up, leaving Trask in a mood that was no longer entirely hopeless.

He should have waited for another call from Grey, but instead, after clearing up several tiresome but essential details on pending cases, he drove out to Grey's house at a clip that made more than one traffic cop do a double take before recognizing the figure at the wheel.

Edgar, a red-haired imp who looked like a mischievous kid fresh from a sandlot infield, but had an I.Q. of 180, admitted him. They were old friends; and if Edgar thought of Trask as a worthy, if not too bright, familiar of his father's—a human shaggy dog—the detective thought of Edgar as a likeable middle-aged genius, masquerading as a boy. Since both played the game, and kept such subversive ideas to themselves, the atmosphere remained genial.

Grey was not so cordial at first; he frowned as Trask came into the big lab. Then his face relaxed, and his mobile lips twitched briefly. It was one of his prime virtues that he seldom forgot the vital difference between young blood, hot and hasty, and his own, rather older, and cooled by rigorous training.

"As it happens, you're not too early—quite," he said, leaning back in the wheelchair.

"Then your idea did pay off!" Trask exclaimed, his face glowing. "What did you learn from the jacket? It's been driving me nuts all day, trying to guess."

"It occurred to me," Grey said, "that a hotel, what with cooking needs and the prevalence of drip-dry syndromes among the guests, would use soft water, especially in this area, where it's normally fairly hard. I had Edgar check: the Regency Hotel does use soft water."

"Soft water?" Trask repeated doubtfully. "I know the term, but just what does it mean?"

27

"We'll get to that in a minute. The point is, an office building, like Connors', would not be likely to bother. No cooking—just washrooms. Drinking water probably in coolers. Anyhow, I had Edgar get a sample from the Connors building. No water softening used."

He saw that Trask had a question trembling on his lips, and didn't wait to hear it. "Artificially softened water usually contains certain chemicals. Silicates, in this case. They're filtered out—in theory— before the liquid gets to the consumer, but enough traces are bound to remain for special tests. The water that soaked Connors' jacket was hard water—had never been softened. *So it could not possibly have come from the Hotel Regency.*

"My guess is, Whitney filled the flask you hypothesized in the office of the Connors Building where he worked; it would have been silly to carry it from his home. It might even be," he added cautiously, "that you could tie the water directly to his office with spectroscopic tests, but that's hardly necessary, since now his story is proved clearly false. The water did not come from the hotel; so it doesn't really matter where it did come from."

"You're so right!" Trask breathed. "We've got him cold."

"You still have to convince a jury."

"This isn't so involved that any normal person can't follow it," Trask said confidently. "Simple scientific logic."

He gave Edgar a suspicious glance; the imp was grinning. Trask then looked at Grey, who pointed a finger at the boy in mock reproof.

"Don't say it, Edgar. Some jurors *can* follow simple scientific logic—so don't be smug."

"I should have known better," the lieutenant said, almost to himself. "I thought it was hopeless—that even you were stumped this time." He sighed. "Will I ever learn?"

"Don't be silly," Grey snapped. "I'm bound to fail some time."

"I'm glad I won't live to see the day," Trask deadpanned.

The Scientist and the Wife Killer

"This man has murdered three wives in succession," Lieutenant Trask said, almost spitting the words out, so deep was his frustration. "Got away clean with the first two, and now he has the incredible gall to use us—the police—as his alibi."

Cyriack Skinner Grey, former research scientist, now a wheelchair case for life, gave the detective a sympathetic scrutiny, noting that he was obviously tired and badly in need of a shave.

"Sounds like a dirty business," Grey said, thinking briefly, and with a poignant stab of anguish, of his own wife, dead at thirty, at the height of her mature and scintillating beauty. Her wit and sensitivity lived on in their son, Edgar, a red-haired, chunky boy of 14 with an I.Q. of 180, and too much humor to be dehumanized by it. "How did your wife killer escape the gas chamber?"

"The best way—almost the only way—to pull a perfect murder," was Trask's grim reply. "Accidental death. The first wife fell down a steep flight of stairs—tripped at the top, he said; worn carpet. It *could* have happened; the hell of it is, we couldn't prove it didn't—not to a jury's satisfaction. The next one drowned while boating; another accident. He tried to save her, but isn't a good enough swimmer."

"What was the motive—the usual?"

"If you mean money, yes. The first wife didn't have much, but her insurance paid him $25,000, which isn't bad pay from a fifty-year-old foolish woman—cherished for only eighteen months—who didn't know when she was well off. Number Two had some savings—around six thousand dollars—and a house worth another twenty-five or so. Not much insurance—he was too smart to increase it."

"He's intelligent enough to make it simple," Grey said, leaning forward in his chair. It glittered with several dozen gimmicks of his own devising; and Trask watched, fascinated, as the scientist fingered some almost invisible controls. There was a faint hum, and the chair's seat tilted to a more comfortable angle. Then a metal disk set in one arm glowed red-hot, and Grey lit a thin, very dark cigar from a humidor that swiveled in front of him and opened smoothly to reveal its contents.

"What's the probability of losing three wives all by accident?" the lieutenant asked. "Pretty small, I'll bet. Be funny if the guy was innocent."

"The laws of probability," Grey said, frowning a little, "aren't like city ordinances, except in being misunderstood or ignored. On a short-run basis, nothing is quite as unlikely as most people think. Every hand one gets in a game of bridge is—if calculated in advance—just as improbable as a perfect one. Yet there are four in every deal."

He saw Trask's brows knit, and added, "However, that's irrelevant. Tell me about the latest murder—if it is one."

"Just another accident, supposedly. Only this time the fellow got even more brazen. You can fall downstairs accidentally, or drown, but how can you be electrocuted accidentally with no electrical appliance around?"

"I don't follow the 'no appliance' point."

"She was in the bathtub; she was small, the tub was big. Her loving husband, Samuel B. Clayton, phoned her at five thirty—from a safe ten miles away, in Oceanview. He got no answer to repeated rings, so he called the police. Pretty extreme measure, you'd think; most men would go home first, and make sure she wasn't out of the house on an errand, or shopping. Not this bird; he wanted witnesses, and had every reason to expect the worst, having rigged it that way, I'll bet my seniority.

30

"Anyhow, he met one of my cruisers at his door, opened the door with his key, and headed for the bathroom. If that was suspicious in itself, he had an explanation. She always bathed between five and six, for dinner; but, he claimed, she would always answer the phone. As to why he called, he said he wanted to tell her he'd be a little late. Mighty unconvincing, all of it, but more believable for just that reason; he knows a little inconsistency is better than a perfect, prepared story.

"Well, we break down the bathroom door, and she's there, all right—dead in the tub. With anybody else, I'd assume she'd had a heart attack or a stroke; but we know Mr. Clayton, so from then on I play it safe. We guard the bathroom until it can be examined inch by inch—and we watch Clayton, after searching him down to the skin. I'm sticking my neck out a mile—false arrest, the works—but I just can't let this joker get away with it again. Only," Trask added hoarsely, "he is!"

"You *broke down* the bathroom door?" Grey asked, his quick mind jumping to a doubtful point. "And yet she was alone in the house?"

"Yes, I thought of that, too," Trask said ruefully. "Nothing to it. Her sister admitted Mrs. Clayton always locked the bathroom door. Some quirk dating back to when she was a little girl, and her mother didn't believe in privacy."

"I see."

"All right, we learned from the coroner that she'd been dead only a short time. Naturally, Clayton had stayed away from the house all day, with plenty of witnesses to prove it. *But* the medical evidence also pointed to electrocution as the cause of death. I don't know the technical details, but a stopped heart, with no thrombosis or muscle damage, and certain other indications, are compatible with electric shock, and not much else.

"But there wasn't a suspicious thing in the room, in terms of electrical appliances. Gas heat, and a ceiling light that was sealed in tight and hadn't been tampered with. Besides, assuming he'd rigged a wire from one of the outlets near the mirror—only two outlets in the room, by the way—we were right there when the door was crashed, and believe me, Clayton wasn't allowed to touch a thing. In other

31

words, if she was electrocuted, whatever did the job must have vanished before we got there."

"I can't accept that," Grey said quickly. "There are other ways to get electric current into a room."

"Agreed. And when Clayton beat us to the basement for a minute, I figured that was the answer."

"You mean he was allowed to go down to the basement—alone?"

"Hold on," the lieutenant interrupted, raising one hand. "It's not like you think. He claimed he had to adjust the hot-water heater—that it had been giving trouble and might even explode. He started down, and I motioned Sergeant Baker to follow. Well, it was dark—Clayton said the bulb must be shot. He grabbed a flashlight from near the top of the stairs, and scooted down.

"Baker followed as fast as he could without knowing the place, and it's cluttered enough, as we found out later. Baker was even quick enough to use his cigarette lighter. I figure Clayton had only a few seconds at the most down there before my man was at his elbow. For those few seconds the flashlight was all over the place, Baker says, but what Clayton did, I just don't know."

"I'll tell you what he did," Grey said in a dry voice. He pressed a button, and as an ashtray appeared like a Martian mouth, gaping on one arm of the wheelchair, Grey deposited an inch of fine snowy ash in it. "He disposed of the gimmick he used to kill his wife—that's what he did."

"I doubt it," Trask said stoutly. "Let me tell you why. We soon replaced the bulb, and had a good look around; after which the crime lab boys did an encore, in spades. There's nothing in that basement but heavy BX cable. If he'd cut into any of that, we'd've found traces—he couldn't possibly cover *them* up in a few seconds. Like you, I thought, what the hell, he ran a wire to the main drainpipe, which is in contact with the water in the tub at the drainage outlet. That would explain the whole *modus operandi* nicely.

"Only, as I said, every power line down there is in BX cable, and I assure you that none of it was tampered with. Now the fuse boxes are outside the house, so don't start thinking—as I did, damn it—that he just ran a line and screw plug from one of the fuse boxes to the drainpipe. He was alone in the basement for just seconds—that's all."

"I congratulate you," the scientist said, smiling wryly. "So far, your logic seems very sound indeed. If no current was tapped in the bathroom, or in the basement—" He stopped, and his eyes narrowed briefly. "Did you check to make sure the tub wasn't still hot—electric-hot, not water-hot—when you got there?"

"Not intentionally," the lieutenant admitted, with a grimace. "But when we hauled her out, if the tub had still been drawing current, and on that wet floor—"

"Of course," Grey said, his eyes hard. "You'd have had a bad shock yourselves—might even have been killed. So," he added thoughtfully, "if he somehow used a gadget, he accomplished the remarkable feat of having it work long enough to kill her, and then disappear without his touching it. A very ingenious fellow—unless he is innocent." The last conclusion didn't sound wholehearted.

"Quite a fellow all around," Trask said, his face looking suddenly older. "If he gets away with it again, he'll not only have her money, but also my hide, all neatly nailed out to dry. I can hardly survive a false arrest suit for a hundred thousand bucks, which he swears to start unless I release him at once—which was several days ago!"

"So you held him. Was that wise?"

"Very unwise; but when I saw his fox face, full of gloating and a kind of malice, all but laughing at us out loud—oh, I know a cop shouldn't get emotional, but from all accounts his wives were pretty nice people. Desperately lonely and pitiful, but they didn't deserve Sam Clayton. I figured—or hoped—we'd find the gimmick that did it. I still don't see how we could have missed it. And that's why," he added fervently, "I'm on your back again."

Trask fixed anxious eyes on the scientist. "Tell me, do you see anything I missed—any possible angle? I've gone over everything in my mind a thousand times. I'm beginning to wonder if we've been hounding an innocent man who happens to look like a fox that's just cleaned out a henhouse."

"All BX cable," Grey murmured. "Not the telephone line, surely. I never heard of BX cable on that."

"No, you're right; the phone line comes up from the basement. But I was thinking only about powerful leads. You know, there isn't enough current in a phone to jolt a flea. And there was no jack in the bathroom to be gimmicked from another line with 110 volts. Not that you could do much with high voltage to a phone; it's ninety per cent insulator—rubber or plastic."

"No jack in the bathroom—hmm! I was wondering about that, but you just eliminated it."

"Then you don't see a glimmer yet?" Trask asked, disappointment edging his voice.

"Afraid not. But neither have I seen the spot."

"But you can't—" the lieutenant blurted, and wrenched his gaze away from the wheelchair.

"Of course, I can't," Grey said cheerfully. "But Edgar can. He's not quite mature or trained enough for all the plausible inferences, but as an observer, he has the sharpest eyes anybody could ask for. Edgar will have a look at the place and then report back to me. Is that all right with you?"

"You bet it is," Trask said. "I know your son is really a fifty-year-old Ph.D. midget," he grinned weakly, "but I won't tell anyone."

The scientist's eyes twinkled.

"If he didn't know more than most Ph.D.'s, I wouldn't let him near my equipment, much less let him be my legs and eyes. Did you know," he asked, "that he's made a small but useful—and entirely original—dent in the Four Color Problem?"

"The which?"

"It's been conjectured, but not proved, that any map—except for some bizarre types with corridors that don't matter—can be colored with just four different colors, so that no two countries sharing a boundary are the same color. Well, Edgar, at only fourteen—" He broke off, and gave a dry little cough. "I'll tell you about it some other time. Right now—" He pressed a button on his control board, and seconds later a buzzer sounded under his chair. "Edgar'll be right down. Will you take him over, and let him look around?"

"With pleasure," Trask said, his face losing some of its haggard tightness.

When the redheaded boy came down, Grey said, "Son, go with the lieutenant. He'll tell you the kind of electrical gadget we're hunting for. I want you to go over the bathroom and basement particularly, and make a note of anything odd—any kind of discrepancy. Look sharp, lad—it's important."

"Gotcha, Dad," was the nonchalant reply. He touched Grey's shoulder—a brief, fleeting tap of affection—and his father seemed to glow for a moment. Then the boy and the detective left, leaving Grey alone in his wheelchair.

At the Clayton house Trask watched with a kind of wry respect as the boy, five feet of curiosity, apparently nuclear-powered, went over the bathroom, with special attention to the two wall outlets and the bathtub's piping.

In the basement, their next stop, Edgar peered at the mass of junk—old barrels, cartons, tools, trunks—and exclaimed, "Brother, what a mess this is!" Then he got to work, concentrating again on all electrical wiring. He scrutinized the BX cable, and admitted grudgingly that the crime lab must be right—it couldn't possibly have been cut or spliced in less than twenty to thirty minutes.

He then used a battery and some meters to check electrical continuity up to the tub—that is, he sent a small current through the main sewer pipe, into which the tub drained, and verified that the metal rim where the plug was seated did get "hot."

"A good jolt sent through that pipe," he told Trask airily, gesturing to the heavy cylinder that crossed a corner of the basement before burrowing into the foundation, "would reach the water in the bathtub, all right."

"Sure," the lieutenant said, trying to keep his tired eyes from closing. "Except that there's no place here to get a good jolt from—except the BX, and everybody, including you, agrees that's not been used."

Holding a powerful police flashlight, the boy was now examining a black rubber-covered wire that came in through a hole alongside the window, went up to the ceiling, and finally through another hole, presumably to the living room.

"That's the telephone wire," Trask told him. "Not enough current in there to feel, even."

"I know," was the calm reply. "But Dad said to look at everything electrical—and what he says, he means."

Edgar had a fine little achromatic doublet in his other hand, and was going over every inch of the phone wire. Trask watched blearily, already seeing himself in court, flattened with a judgment of more money than he could earn in a lifetime. False arrest. No right to hold Clayton; previous "accidents" neither admissible nor relevant. Scratch one police lieutenant—killed by a fox.

The boy gave a little squeal of excitement, and Trask stiffened.

"What is it?" he snapped.

"*This* wire's been tampered with—I think."

"You think! Look, Edgar, I gotta go into court—anyhow, it's only a phone wire. So why waste time—?"

"Dad said—"

"Never mind!" the detective groaned. "Let me see."

Through the clear, glowing lens of the doublet he was able to make out two punctures in the rubber insulation. They didn't suggest much to him.

"There are gadgets to cut in that don't need strippers or tape," the boy said. "They just send two sharp prongs through the insulation— quick like a bunny."

"Not enough current, damn it!" the exasperated Trask roared. "Those blasted holes may have been there for years, anyhow."

"No, they're new," Edgar said. "Maybe they don't mean anything, but, as Dad always says, first catch your data—it was 'hare' originally, you know."

"I don't know, confound it," the detective groaned again. "But never let it be said I lack faith. I don't have any idea what your father and you are up to, but I'm hoping hard—brother, am I hoping!"

Forty minutes later, his inspection complete, Edgar led the way out. Trask dropped him at Grey's house, and half asleep, said wearily, "Ask your dad to call me if he makes sense out of your report. It certainly doesn't mean anything to me." And he drove off.

Usually he was hopeful, because Grey had a genius for breaking tough cases—a combination of solid scientific training and an almost poetic imagination. But this time—perhaps because he was so exhausted and worried—Trask considered himself sunk.

The next morning—not too early, since Grey must have guessed how badly the lieutenant needed sleep—there was a call. It brought Trask to the scientist's house as fast as a cruiser, with siren wailing, could get him there.

So anxious was the detective that he almost forgot his manners, and barely managed to say hello before showering questions on Grey.

"Slow down," the scientist advised him gently. "I'll tell you everything I know—and some I've guessed, pretty wildly, but I feel, accurately."

"Don't tell me it was the phone wire, because we both know—"

"I will tell you," Grey said a bit sharply. "If you'll let me. Yes, it was the phone wire."

Trask opened his mouth to protest, met the scientist's level gaze, and closed it again.

"I will admit," Grey said, "it was news to me, too. But I make a point of checking things out, and talked to a repairman—a phone company expert. It's true that a conversation on a telephone is carried by a very tiny current. But what most people—including us—don't know, is that the *ringing* is another story. That takes about a hundred volts."

Trask gaped at him.

"A hundred volts! Why, that's as dangerous as a regular power line."

"Exactly. Clayton must have run a lead from the phone wire to the sewer pipe, which Edgar tells me is only eighteen inches away, using a quick splice that just pierces the insulation. At the pipe he either just wrapped the hot lead around the metal, or perhaps used a small alnico magnet to hold it there. Then, when he had a few seconds in the dark later, all he had to do was tug the lead free and toss it into some barrel or carton. He rightly figured that you'd suspect the BX, but finding it intact, would never dream a phone line was even involved."

Trask was silent a moment.

"Then his phone call—the mere ringing—actually killed her," he said in a shaken voice. "He knew she'd be in the tub when the phone rang."

"If she wasn't—then—he'd've called again," Grey said, his face stern. "However, I don't know how you can make out a case, even now."

"First we'll find that lead. He's already admitted the call, so we know the exact time of death. Then there's the punctured insulation. I can break him down, I'm sure; he won't expect we figured out his gimmick. But even if he holds out, there's enough for a jury. It all fits—the ringing of the phone call, his running down to the basement, the coroner's report—and that wire lead with prongs to match the holes in the rubber insulation. Oh, we'll trap that little fox this time!"

"I'm sure you will," Grey said grimly.

The Scientist and the Vanished Weapon

Lieutenant Trask's face was grey and haggard, not so much from fatigue—he'd had only four hours' sleep in the last two days, which was no more than usual—as from frustration, grief, and rage.

"This is the season of miracles," he said in a bitter voice. "Christmas, Peace on Earth, Love Thy Neighbor, and all the rest. But I didn't expect a teenage killer to pull a miracle. Drucker had a wife and four children," he added, "and this punk Remick shot three slugs into poor Drucker before Tom even knew what was happening. It didn't have to be like that; the punk could've got out the back door easily; Drucker was big and slow. Brave—too damned brave—but slow. I told him a million times to stop taking chances—to have his gun out and to use it, but not Tom—always afraid he'd shoot a frightened kid. Now," Trask grated, "one shot him—three times over. He might've lived—probably would've, Doc says—if Remick hadn't fired twice more."

Cyriack Skinner Grey, sitting quietly in the wheelchair in which he was destined to stay for the rest of his life, felt a surge of affection and sympathy for the tired detective. The police often suffered from a bad image in the public eye, but there were thousands of fine men like Trask who killed themselves by inches—when they didn't die violently at the hands of criminals—trying to make life safer for the people of their communities.

Grey took a shot-glass from a recess in one arm of the chair, held it under a tiny tap, and pressed a button. Amber liquid flowed out in a thin stream. He held the drink up for his friend.

"Can't," Trask said regretfully. "I'm still on duty."

The older man cocked his head, shrugged, and drank the whiskey himself.

"In that case," he said, "how about some coffee?"

From another faucet he quickly produced a hot, black, and fragrant brew, drawing it into a small handleless cup of fine bone china.

Trask shook his head in wonder, and accepted it.

"One of these days," he said, a little of the gloom leaving his face, "you'll haul a beautiful dancing girl out of that incredible contraption, and that's when I'll have myself tested for hallucinations!" He knew that Grey, formerly a top research scientist, who still had a fully equipped lab in this old house, had built a hundred gadgets into his wheelchair; yet the lieutenant was surprised by a new one at least once a month. But it was because of the old man's flair for solving problems, first in the lab and now as a freelance crime consultant, that Trask had come to see him.

"All right," Grey said, as the detective swallowed a third cupful. "Let's have it. What's all this about a miracle?"

"The miracle of the vanishing gun," Trask said. "I was licked at the scene, but I figured if anybody could counter a bad miracle with a good one, you're the man to do it."

He gave Grey the empty cup, and with hands clasped behind his back, paced the floor of the old man's study, speaking as he walked.

"It's like this. Tom Drucker caught the kid—Arnold Remick's his full name—inside Jack's Camera Exchange. The punk saw Tom first, and put three slugs into him; then he ran. Two of my men were in a cruiser not far away; they heard the shots and poured it on to get there. They spotted Remick going down an alley, and took after him. The punk hopped a fence, so they left the car to follow. The kid was running scared, I guess, because he ducked into a big apartment building and up the stairs. Fool thing to do really—no way out.

"Well, he sees an apartment with the door ajar, and slips in; but my two men, right behind, catch a glimpse, and know they have him boxed.

"The kid was kill-crazy; he fired right through the door until he ran out of shells. That's my guess, anyhow—we don't have the gun yet, which is why I'm here. When he stopped shooting, my men crashed into the place and handcuffed him—there was no more fight left in the punk.

"Naturally, they looked for the gun first thing, but it just wasn't there. The window was open, the way the door had been, and for the same reason. The woman who lives there had something cooking in the oven, so she wanted to air the rooms out. Meanwhile she went downstairs to chew the fat with another woman.

"Not finding the gun in the apartment, the men figure Remick tossed it out the window—what good that would do, I don't think he stopped to consider. He should've known we'd find it below soon enough. That's what *I* thought!" Trask added bitterly. "We combed that yard inch by inch, and every other area reachable from a third-floor window by a pro pitcher—nothing.

"Now you tell me," Trask concluded, jaw out, looking squarely at Grey, "how a jerky kid with only seconds to spare can make a .38 automatic—that's what it was, judging from the bullets they dug out of poor Drucker—vanish. That's what I meant by a punk pulling a miracle."

"Gun not in the apartment—you're sure?"

"Absolutely. Nobody could hide something that big so quickly where we couldn't find it. We tore that place wide open. The tenant didn't like us one bit."

"Is the boy naturally clever or ingenious?"

"Just the opposite, damn it—that's what bugs me. He's a stupid drop-out punk of seventeen—can hardly put a sentence together, even in Basic English. And everything else he did that night shows stupidity—stupidity and hate. And another thing," the lieutenant said in a thoughtful voice, "it just came to me. I think Remick expected us to find the gun. When my man came back empty-handed Remick looked sort of surprised. Now why was that, I wonder?"

"Tell me about the yard."

"Nothing to tell. Wouldn't be much of a sight even in summer—very little gardening done, I imagine. Right now, at this time of the year, it's just bare, except for the two grubby trees, the birdbath, and a barbecue covered with a plastic sheet. Oh, and a wooden table with built-on bench seats—you know the kind; like on a picnic ground."

"You checked them all, of course?"

"You bet. Found exactly nothing. Even took the plastic off the barbecue, although the gun obviously didn't go through it—no hole. And the birdbath was just solid ice inside. Without that gun," he said sourly, "we can't make a case, especially against a juvenile. The punk can claim he was just scared and running for fear of being accused. Sure, we can swear he fired from the room, and produce slugs similar to the ones that killed Tom, but you know juries and lawyers. They'll say: if this kid had a gun, where is it? Oh, you don't have it? Maybe it's just another cop frame-up—swearing away a boy's life because we let the real killer escape."

"What about the area beyond the yard?" Grey asked. He pressed a button; a humidor swung out and swiveled open. He took a thin, very black cigar from it, and the box disappeared with a snake-like glide.

Watching the scientist light the cheroot in a glowing disc set into one arm of the wheelchair, the detective said, "Same story. All pretty bare. Dry fishpond; some scrubby dead grass; a few beat-up shrubs—no place where a gun could disappear."

"Forgive me if I'm obvious," Grey said, smiling crookedly, "but couldn't somebody outside have simply picked it up and carried it away?"

"I thought of that. But the yard is completely fenced in, and it was dark out, remember. A person after the gun would need eyes like an owl, and he'd have to move like a scalded cat, besides. My man got down there pretty fast, after that quick first check of the apartment. We guarded the area all night, and searched again this morning—but no luck."

The scientist sat quietly in his chair, puffing on the cigar.

"I suppose," the detective said a little wistfully, "it's time to call in Edgar."

He meant Grey's puckish carrot-topped son, aged 14, who had an I.Q. of 180 and a genius for higher mathematics, especially topology. His father, who hated prigs, had made sure that Edgar developed both a sense of humor and a large bump of humility. As a widower and an intellectual, he knew the risk of raising his son single-handed but hoped—and planned—for the best. Edgar was the immobilized scientist's legs; he gathered data from which Grey extracted the key patterns that led to the solutions of his cases.

"No-o," Grey drawled. "I don't think that's necessary this time. If you've searched as carefully as you say, then sending Edgar to the scene wouldn't help. It seems to be a matter of pure reason at this point. Considering how quickly Remick must have acted, and assuming that your inference about his own surprise is valid, I can think of only one possible solution."

Trask was staring at him.

"Are you trying to tell me," he blurted, "that you already have it solved? That you know where the gun is?"

"I wouldn't be quite that dogmatic. But if your report was factual and complete, then my solution is at least highly probable. It was a cold night, I believe you said."

"That's right," the detective replied, almost absently. "Damp-cold, with some freezing slush on the ground. Which, by the way, as I should have told you, also indicated that nobody else picked up the gun from the yard and took it away—no fresh footprints except our own. Now," he begged, "for the love of Pete, what's the answer? Where is the gun?"

"I would say," the old man drawled with maddening deliberation, "that the gun is at the bottom of the birdbath, under the ice."

"Wha-a-t?" Trask exclaimed; then his face darkened, and he shook his head emphatically. "It can't be. This time, for once, you're wrong. Maybe it's my fault," he added quickly. "I didn't make the timing clear enough. After my men crashed the door, a fast once-over turned up nothing, so one of them ran down to the yard, while the other kept searching the apartment. Now, Ferber's a good cop; he checked the birdbath— remember this was less than ten minutes after Remick tossed out the gun, if he did. Well, there were six inches of solid ice in that birdbath—solid, as I said."

He gave Grey a weak, lopsided smile. "I'm an old pond-skater from Vermont; I know how water freezes. First, a crust forms at the top; then the ice moves down to the bottom. But it takes quite a while, even in cold weather. Last night it was maybe twenty-eight or so. That birdbath couldn't possibly freeze completely in the few minutes after the kid ditched the gun. And if it broke through the crust, Ferber would have found it—he jabbed the ice, and it was frozen solid right through to the bottom. Besides, the hole the gun would have made going through the crust would show up different, even if it glazed over fast."

"I take it the ice wasn't clear."

"No, dirty."

"So Ferber couldn't see down to the bottom," Grey said placidly.

"No, but—"

"All right," the old man interrupted him, beginning to show impatience. "I see the point you've tried to make. Only it's not necessarily valid in this case. If your search was thorough, the gun's not anywhere in the apartment or on the ground outside. Therefore it must be in the birdbath."

Grey raised one hand as Trask began to protest again. "Ever hear of supercooling? Last night the temperature dropped to below freezing—about twenty-eight, you suggested. Now, ordinarily, water begins to solidify at thirty-two, with very little leeway. But occasionally, when the temperature drop is gradual and the liquid remains undisturbed, it stays unfrozen even with a fall to several degrees below thirty-two. Then, if you toss a pebble, a twig—or a gun—into the supercooled water, it suddenly freezes solid, in a flash, all the way to the bottom.

"I think that's what happened last night. The boy got panicky and tossed the gun out of the window, not knowing how else to get rid of it fast. He *did* expect you to find it, which is why he looked so surprised at your failure. He couldn't guess that it would fall into the supercooled water of the birdbath, triggering it instantaneously to ice. As an old pond-skater," he jibed, "I'm surprised you never noticed the phenomenon before. Anyhow, you'd have found the gun after the first thaw."

Trask was wordless for a moment, then he said, "Not if somebody else—maybe a pal of Remick's tipped off to look around for what we missed—got there first." He wagged his head wonderingly. "Supercooled water—well, I'll be damned. The funny thing is," he said sheepishly, "that it comes back to me now. One night my dad actually showed us the stunt—made the whole pond on our farm freeze instantly by tossing in a stone. But I was only about nine, and didn't remember it till now. I'm almost afraid to check, in case you're wrong."

"If I am," Grey said, "then the boy is either a genuine miracle worker or your men are not very efficient. Why not go and find out," he suggested. "I'm rather curious myself."

"I'll just call Gaffney, who's watching the place," Trask said. "Then we'll know the truth in a hurry."

The answer came back by phone a few minutes later. The gun was there—a .38, and empty.

"It will match those slugs," the lieutenant said, "so now we've got a case."

"Congratulations," the old man said in his driest voice. "And now I'll get back to my electronics."

He pressed a button. A motor hummed in the base of his wheelchair, and it rolled up a ramp toward the lab on the second floor. Trask watched for a moment, smiling, and then headed for the door. Suddenly the smile left his mouth. He still had to face Mrs. Drucker and Tom's four kids.

The Scientist and the Obscene Crime

"Mr. Neil Burnett here has a problem the police can't lick," Lieutenant Trask admitted unhappily. "We're trying, and officially I wouldn't call it defeat, but …" He shrugged.

The man in the wheelchair, where he was destined to spend the rest of his life, gave the detective a brief, wry smile, and then scrutinized the young man. He noted the haggard face, the greenish pouches under the dark eyes, and the quivering tenseness of his too-thin body.

"Relax, my boy," Grey said in his resonant voice, which usually had a soothing effect. A former research scientist of great brilliance and imagination, he still worked in a fine home laboratory financed from his valuable patents; but, in addition, he had become a crime consultant to Trask, an early pupil of his. "You won't help matters by coming apart. When did you last get a good night's sleep—or a square meal?"

"I can't remember," was the bitter reply. "Between Laura's trouble—that's the reason I'm here—and my work at medical school it's been rough. Only a year to go, and then suddenly this—this crazy, filthy business. And it's happening to us!"

Cyriack Skinner Grey was not only a scientist but a gentleman; he had a large bump of compassion, especially for the young. He took a shot-glass from a recess under the arm of his wheelchair, which was studded with gadgets of his own devising—mainly electronic—and from a tiny tap alongside drew a generous portion of amber liquid. He handed the drink to Neil Burnett.

"Try this," he said. "It will do you good."

The young man hesitated only for a few seconds, then gulped down the drink. He blinked, coughed, and a faint grin touched his lips.

"Wow!" he said. But clearly, some of the tension was gone.

"What's it all about?" Grey asked, turning now to the lieutenant.

"Obscene phone calls," Trask said tightly. "Some psychopath has been annoying Miss Nolan, Neil's fiancée. Horrible stuff. She's no prude, but there's a limit."

"You must have a suspect. Usually the caller knows his victim, and may even have a known grudge."

"Better than that—it's more than a suspicion. Laura knows who's doing it; so do I; but proving it's another story. Just a voice over the phone. Undoubtedly it's Leo Fenton. He worked in the same office with her for a while, and pestered her for dates. She's engaged to Neil here, and naturally turned him down. She couldn't stand him anyhow; he made her skin crawl. Everybody knew before very long that he was sick. They had to bounce him out. Then these filthy calls began."

Grey gave Burnett an owlish stare.

"Since you know who's doing it, why not look him up and—ah—dissuade him? From the size of your shoulders I'd say you could throw a pretty good punch."

"Now, wait a minute—!" Trask objected, but Burnett cut in quickly.

"It's not that simple, as the lieutenant was about to explain. Years ago it would have worked fine. But today, if you clout anybody, no matter what he does—even pushing your grandmother into a mudhole—it means going to court. I can't risk that now. I'm in my final year, with a good record and good prospects. A conviction for assault, or any bad publicity for the school, would ruin me. They wouldn't care a damn whose fault it was. There's an image to protect," he added in a dry voice.

"All right," Grey said. "I withdraw the suggestion. Why doesn't she leave her job—go where he can't find her?"

"She may have to," was the gloomy reply. "But Laura is private and personal secretary to the president of the company. It took five tough years for her to make it, and that was fast, but she's very bright. Frankly, we need the money. It will take me some time, even after I'm graduated and finish interning, to build up any kind of practice, and Laura's carrying the load. I can't do outside work and go to med school," he pointed out. "If she took another job, it would be a piddling one in comparison, and we need every cent to get along."

"What about screening her calls through another girl?"

"They tried that," the young man said. "Fenton's too sly, too clever. He can change his voice whenever he wants to—pretend to be somebody else, or some big shot's male secretary. So he manages to get through most of the time, and always talks dirty. Laura hangs up as fast as she can, but still it's no fun. He always ends with: 'Say something sweet, baby—I'm waiting.' And he does wait—you can hear him breathing. Then he gives a crazy, giggling laugh, and click! he's gone. Of course, she never gives him time to finish, but he can spew out a lot of obscenity in a hurry, and she's stunned—like a bird with a snake, she says."

"He calls from pay phones," Trask explained, "and never uses the same one twice. We've put tails on him, hoping to catch him in the act, and have him committed for psychiatric examination, but he's too smart. Always goes through department stores or busy supermarkets where a man—or even two—can't stay close to him. Then he scoots out through a side door. Following him from home has been a bust."

"So you see what we're up against," Neil said glumly. "We know who's doing it, and the police can pick him up almost any time at his apartment; but they say there's no case. Laura has a wonderful job, and has to take a lot of calls—that's one of her main functions: sweet-talking people too important to be brushed off, but not quite big enough for J.M., her boss, to bother with."

48

Grey looked thoughtful. He pressed a button on the arm of his wheelchair; a humidor slid out of a recess and swiveled into a handy position. The scientist selected a thin, very black cigar, and the humidor glided back out of sight. He touched something else, and a circular patch glowed red-hot on the other arm of the wheelchair. He held the cigar against it until fragrant blue smoke arose, then put the cigar to his lips.

"Get any tapes?" he asked Trask.

"Several."

"Anybody try to match them against Fenton's voice?"

"Yes, the crime lab had a go at it, but the results weren't conclusive. The squiggles were similar, but it seems a psychopath isn't consistent even in his speech patterns or wave lengths or whatever's involved. A good lawyer—hell, even a punk one—would murder the D.A. in court. Besides, let's face it: the D.A. doesn't think the case is very important compared with the murders, hit and runs, and assaults we're getting."

"If we could only squirt some dye down the phone wire," Burnett said, with a weak grin; the liquor was acting on his empty stomach, Grey inferred, feeling a pang of guilt. "All over Fenton's big flabby face—that might prove he was the one, even to the dumbest jury."

"Mark him with gentian violet, hey?" the scientist said. "Pity it's not a voice tube; you'd have the solution. A definite label … hmm."

"It's pretty hopeless," Burnett said. "We're just wasting your time, I'm afraid. But the lieutenant said that if anybody could find a solution, you could."

"Trask overrates me," Grey said a little sharply. "I've bungled more than once. However, give me a chance to think about it. I have the vague glimmering of the ghost of an idea—it's that tenuous. Let me have your phone number, and the one at Laura's office." He touched another button; a clipboard slid out like magic, and he pulled a sheet of paper off the top. "Write on that."

When Neil had done so, Grey squinted at the writing, and said dryly, "You should be a good doctor—your scribble is almost indecipherable! Now get some sleep. Trask or I will let you know if anything useful occurs to us."

When Trask and Burnett had left, the old man settled down in his wheelchair, puffing at the black cigar. He was trying to lure some unformed idea from the fringes of his consciousness to where he could grasp it. He was intrigued by Neil's quip about pouring dye down the phone wire; it seemed related somehow to the solution he was seeking.

Three days later Burnett, Trask, and two other detectives converged on the main switchboard outside of Laura's office. With them was Grey's assistant and legman—his impish, red-haired 14-year-old son with an I.Q. of 180 and the good sense not to take it too seriously. After Grey had matured some theoretical ideas about a case, it was usually up to Edgar to implement them, under Trask's questioning eyes.

Ordinarily, Laura would have been inside, at her desk, which guarded the boss's door; but Grey preferred to have the call intercepted at the main board; so she had been "demoted" for the day and was holding down a job that had preceded her rise in the firm.

There was no telling when Fenton would call, but of late he tended to pick early afternoons. In any case, they had no choice but to sweat it out.

"Remember," Trask told Laura, "you're to wait until he says 'Say something sweet, baby'—then hand Edgar the headset in a hurry." He looked at one of his men. "Is Fenton's apartment staked out?"

"Yes, sir. If he comes back there from the pay phone, he'll be grabbed. Think he will?"

"I don't see why not," the lieutenant said. "Unless he knows what Grey is up to—which is more than I do," he complained, giving Edgar a reproachful glance.

Luckily, they didn't have to wait long. At 2:18 Laura answered a call, and they saw her stiffen, first flushing deeply, then becoming very pale. Burnett swore, his hands tightening into fists, as he noted her expression of revulsion.

Edgar stood near her; in his hand was a cylindrical object with a flared mouth. It was the size of a small water glass, and two bare copper wires projected from the base. Somehow word had spread to other offices, and a crowd had collected. Even the president came out of his lordly isolation; he was like a sheepdog hustled by an unruly flock.

Laura suddenly slipped the headset off and passed it to Edgar. He took it, placed the flared end of his tubular metal device against the mouthpiece, and deftly made the two copper wires touch.

There was a startlingly loud detonation, so sharp and whiplike that it caused the spectators' ears to ring, even though they were ten yards away.

"Dad concentrated on those frequencies best carried by the phone," Edgar said airily. "It has a pretty limited range, you know, but we hit Fenton mighty hard in the middle of it. Dad doesn't think his eardrum will break, but he should be deaf in one ear for several hours. If you pick him up, and have the police surgeon test his hearing—with witnesses—you should have a case that will satisfy the D.A."

"We're on our way." Trask was smiling grimly, and his eyes were no longer questioning.

The Scientist and the Multiple Murder

An experienced police officer, like a doctor, is not easy to shock. A few highway accidents, with men, women, and children reduced to bloody tatters, will usually immunize the cop or impel him to change his profession.

Lieutenant Trask had been through the mill—murder, narcotics, arson, vice, and sex crimes—but the sight awaiting him on the roof of the Ashcroft Building sent a spurt of acid up from his tightening stomach, and into his gullet.

Part of it was owing to the contrast: a perfect summer night, warm, balmy, and clear, with thousands of stars blazing brightly overhead; the huge luxurious swimming pool, illuminated only by underwater flood lights, and glowing greenish-blue; and in the translucent liquid, eight dead men—six on the bottom; one, by some quirk of body fat, floating face down on the surface; and the eighth somehow caught by one arm in the magnesium ladder at the side.

Trask took a deep breath and swallowed the acid phlegm in his mouth. He turned to the white-haired little man with him, and said, "They told me you reported 'something wrong' up on the roof—to bring a doctor—but this ..." He shook his head. "What in hell happened here?"

"I dunno," the watchman said, almost in a whisper. "That's how I found 'em half an hour ago—eleven thirty, it was. I wondered why they was stayin' up here so late. It was just supposed to be an hour or two—that's what Mr. Logan said, anyhow."

"Some kind of meeting?"

"Sort of. They was kinda celebratin', I guess. The offices closed at five, like always; but the top brass, they came up here for a swim; it was such a fine night, Mr. Logan said. 'We're gonna celebrate our victory,' I heard him say." He peered at the detective from watery blue eyes. "What d'ya think happened, Lieutenant?"

"Offhand, I'd say they must have been electrocuted by some short in those lights. But we'll know more when the coroner gets here. It had better be an accident," he added darkly. "I hate to think of anything else. Eight at one blow—like that old fairy tale about a tailor."

"Huh?"

"Nothing," Trask said shortly. He knew he had no business speculating in front of the watchman, but after all the fellow was a kind of cop, and although the detective wouldn't admit it, the sight of that pool with eight corpses in it had shaken him.

He stepped to the edge and very gingerly dipped one finger in the water, squatting to do so. There was no telltale tingling to indicate that the liquid was charged. If there had been a short, it had cured itself.

"Did any fuses blow?" he asked the old man. "Or circuit breakers kick in and out?"

"Didn't see anything. Nary a flicker."

Trask walked to the ladder, and took a closer look at the man dangling there, one arm between the rungs just above the water level. Then he had that feeling—zero at the bone—and knew accidental death was no longer very likely.

The dead man had a wound in his back, just below the right shoulder. It looked as if some jagged instrument had been jabbed in and then pulled out. Further data would have to come from the coroner—where the devil was Doc Kendall? He should be here by now.

The lieutenant scrutinized the bottom of the pool. No radio had fallen in—or been thrown in. Besides, up here, any set was almost sure to be a battery transistor model, safe in or out of the pool.

"Did anybody else come up here tonight?" he asked the watchman, who was whistling tunelessly between his teeth. They clicked when he spoke; obviously the old man wore dentures.

"Nobody else. The main door was locked; the alarms were set. Besides, Mrs. Dvorak and her women were cleaning the top floor. He'd have to get past them, too, and that old bag never misses nothin' around here at night."

"No elevator up here?"

"Stops at the floor just below. Then there's a private stairway for the big shots to use this pool. Mrs. Dvorak was workin' there. She didn't see nobody—I already ast her."

"Why'd you do that?" Trask demanded, suspicion in his voice.

"Waal, it's like this. Any time there's trouble, who catches hell, mister? Watchman, that's who. Got the whole dummed place to guard at night—twenty-six floors—and only two hands. But I'll catch hell for this, no matter how it happened."

"Then you weren't up here?"

"Not until Mrs. Dvorak called down and said things was awful quiet all of a sudden. She was afraid to look; Mr. Logan's a hard man, and if he thought she was snoopin'—so I come up. It *was* funny, them stayin' up here so late—near midnight."

"And you found them—like this. Touch anything?"

"You bet not. I was a sheriff once myself—retired five years ago. Sherman City, Illinois. Sheriff for twenty-nine years. Ran a clean town, too."

"Been here ever since?"

"Almost. Four years, eight months yesterday. Not much of a job, but you don't get any big pensions as an ex-lawman, hey?"

Trask began to make a circuit of the roof. There wasn't much else he could do until the coroner came. It was beginning to look as if accidental death might be the answer after all. If nobody else had been up here ... of course, one of the swimmers might have bungled the job and been caught in his own murder trap. Not likely, the detective told himself glumly.

His walk around the parapet was no help. There was only one building for blocks that matched this one in height; it stood several stories taller, and was about 150 feet away. All the others, while closer, were pygmies in comparison, the tallest having only 15 floors or so.

He thought about a climb from a lower window of this tower. That would certainly bypass the cleaning women. But the killer would still have to get into the building somehow, and keep clear of the watchman and alarm system. Or he could have hidden out during office hours, Trask reminded himself.

He visualized the sides of the tower. They were all of modern aluminum and glass construction. The place was a typical city aiguille that would baffle an expert alpinist. He couldn't see the killer—if there was one—hammering pitons into the aluminum panels and inching his way to the roof.

Knock it off, he told himself sternly. Cause of death is still unknown—you're just shadow boxing.

"Wow!" somebody exclaimed softly behind him, and the lieutenant whirled. It was the coroner, a tall lean man, never known to wear an expression other than sorrowful, even though he was an outrageous punster.

Trask gave him a terse summary of the situation to that moment. Coroner Kendall pursed his lips, wagging his big head.

"Homicide, I know—and suicide. Would you call this 'octicide,' my friend?" He moved nearer to the pool. "We'll have to get them out. I can't swim, and wouldn't want my observations—ah—watered down."

The detective groaned. "I'll have some men here soon. There's a sort of boathook over there; it shouldn't be too hard."

"Man's the highest form of life," Kendall said, "but this business of splashing around twenty-six stories up is carrying things to an extreme. And at midnight, yet."

"They hadn't planned to stay this late," the lieutenant said. "My guess is they were dead for quite a while before the watchman got up here."

"Just offhand," the coroner said, "it has to be electrocution. What else could kill all eight, and not a man to climb out?"

"The one by the ladder has a wound," Trask told him.

"So I see. But he didn't get it from the ladder. Smooth metal; no blood or tissue that I can see. Hmm. Short circuit, I suppose—not that that explains the injury; just the deaths."

"We'll see," was Trask's curt reply.

But the lieutenant had an uneasy feeling that he was up against a locked-room case of the classic sort. Before this is over, he told himself unhappily, I'll be calling on Grey again.

Cyriack Skinner Grey, formerly a research scientist, and now a wheelchair case for life, was enjoying a new career as a crime consultant. His huge rambling house had a fine laboratory, paid for from his many valuable patents; his wheelchair was a constellation of ingenious gadgets, ranging from taps for hot coffee and cold martinis to swiveling humidors, remote control hi-fi, and—as Trask once remarked—everything but instant dancing girls.

He could not investigate crimes on the scene, but his son, Edgar, a puckish fourteen-year-old redhead with an I.Q. of 180, had sharp eyes, strong legs and the good judgment not to be priggish about any of these. He was Grey's five senses—and a lot more, now that the old man was a widower.

"It seems to be murder," Trask told him, after a summary of the case. It was a well-organized recapitulation, since the lieutenant had once been a pupil of Grey's, and had learned something about delivering a good précis. "We tested the lights; they're the best, perfectly sealed and waterproof. Not the slightest leakage of current. That, and the wound, which nobody can explain, are the things. Baker—the wounded man—was certainly uninjured before going to the roof; his wife saw him about four. It's not the kind of gash a man could easily hide. Made just about the time of death, the coroner thinks; that's why so little blood flowed."

"What's the motive—if it was murder? Must be something mighty big to make someone kill eight people at one stroke."

"They had it coming, in a way. But how it was done—that's what gets me. To make it short, they froze Ashcroft out of his own company—him and a few supporters, including his sons. What makes it worse, they all owed him their jobs and success. Damned ingrates, apparently."

"What kind of business is it?"

"Importers. Ashcroft brought in the best from England, stood behind it, and was satisfied with a fair profit. But the fast-buck boys in the organization saw ways to make a killing—cheap, flashy stuff, sold by trading on the Ashcroft name. Look," Trask said, "we've done a lot of spade work and are pretty sure of the possible suspects—in a way, that is. But it's a vicious circle. Without knowing how, we can't settle on who, and vice versa."

He knew how the outburst sounded, flushed, and said, "Let me get at it by telling you about Ashcroft and his family."

"Go right ahead," Grey said, his lips twitching briefly. He pressed a stud on one arm of his chair and a humidor swung out; the top of the humidor rose smoothly, and he took out a thin, very dark cigar, whereupon the box slid out of sight into some recess. He lit the cheroot from a disk that glowed cherry-red at the touch of another button.

"Ashcroft's father came here from England as a boy. He was the youngest son, the estate was mortgaged to the limit, and there were six other children ahead of him. It's a very old and honorable family, by the way.

"Anyhow, William Ashcroft did well, and the present one, Edward, even better, building up the importing company. Edward has four children—his wife died a few years ago. His daughter lives in France, married to a painter; she wasn't well enough to come. The three sons all came—oh, Lord! I didn't mention that Ashcroft had a stroke after he was frozen out; that's why the kids came.

"They all think the world of him, except Harry; he never saw eye to eye with his father on the business. The boy was full of the family tradition—the old man's mistake—and wanted him to buy back the ancestral estate and live on the land like country gentlemen. It wasn't practicable, naturally; most of the place is government controlled now—historic home bit. But Harry was bitter, and lives as best he can—won't take any of his father's money. Teaches history at some fancy school, I understand.

"The other two sons are with the company—or were. They got pushed out with Ashcroft. So you can see there's plenty of motive."

"Yes," Grey said slowly. "But killing eight men is a pretty wild and extravagant act."

"I know. But after going into all the backgrounds, I can't see anybody but an Ashcroft as the killer. The others who got the ax just aren't the sort to respond that way. But I must admit that none of the Ashcrofts, father or sons, can be placed on the roof. Which is why I'm here. I need your ideas on how the killer got to the roof, past the cleaning women and watchman, and electrified that pool."

"There must be outlets up there."

"Sure. He could plug in a cord, bare the ends, and drop the stripped part in the water. But how did he get up there? And where did he go afterwards? And where's the wire?"

"Let's check the facts," Grey said. "They began this celebration after a few rounds of drinks and some dinner—about eight, you said?"

"Right."

"When they didn't come down, and things were too quiet at about eleven thirty, the watchman had a look, and that's when the bodies were found?"

"Right again."

"And the nearby buildings are out—either well below or too far away. What about climbing from a lower window?"

"There aren't any as such. The place is air-conditioned; the windows are glass-brick, and don't open."

Grey was silent, blowing a cloud of fragrant blue smoke toward the ceiling. Then he said, "Why no women at the roof party?"

"It wasn't that kind of a thing—just an informal affair, with some business to settle, too. The real bash, with wives and girl friends, was set for later in the week."

"One point is important. Was this an impromptu get-together, or could the killer have known in advance?"

"It was pretty well spread around early in the week that on Friday night the top brass were scheduled to have drinks and dinner right after work, and then meet on the roof—if the weather was right. You know," Trask added, "if they had included some of their women, that might've saved them. The killer might hesitate to kill wives; they're not directly part of the dirty work."

"I wonder," the scientist said. "Remember that not all the men were equally guilty, either. It was a ruthless crime—bordering on the insane, I should say."

"Wish I could give you more, but it's mainly a matter of how, as I said. I brought dossiers on the Ashcrofts. The old boy has quite a place—twenty acres, at least. The house is like an English country place. You know, the family goes back centuries. They showed me a dagger given to Sir Walter Ashcroft by the Black Prince at Crecy, and there's armor, weapons, heraldic devices—a lot of such stuff. But, damn it, I don't know which of the three did it. Ashcroft himself is in the clear—paralyzed on one side ever since the Board of Directors meeting knifed him in the back. Likewise the daughter—she's still in France, and pretty sick; I checked with the Sûreté.

"But the three sons—now, there's the rub. They make no bones about hating Hewitt Logan—he was the ringleader behind it all—and the ones who backed him. They all have hot, fierce eyes—the younger Ashcrofts. I gather their father dinned it into them about the family honor and all the famous knights in their genealogy. Later, when he saw how seriously Harry took it, he may have been sorry he laid it on so thick."

"Well," Grey said. "There isn't really much I can do now. I haven't a glimmer of an idea so far. I'd better study all these documents, and try to get oriented."

"Just figure out *how*—you're the man for that. Once I know how it was done, I should be able to pick the who. The cleaning woman, Dvorak, and all the others I grilled, seemed to have nothing to hide, and the old gal didn't miss much. She says nobody came by her to the roof, so you'll have to figure out how she's mistaken, or if there's another way—which is impossible, as I see it. A real locked-room case, that's what it is!"

"I'll think about it," the old man said soothingly. "If I get any notions, I may send Edgar up there to look around."

"Be my guest—the sight of that red-headed fifty-year-old dwarf on the job will be more than welcome, believe me," Trask said in a fervent voice, and left.

Thereafter, for an unhappy, fruitless week, Trask chased his own tail, as he put it, with the D.A. and the press baying at his heels. After all, eight men—all over forty thousand a year in salaries—were dead, presumably by murder. And no word of any break in the case—no clue, no key suspect, no arrest. It was beginning to appear, the detective reflected in dismay, as if even Grey himself was stumped at last.

Then he got a cryptic call from the scientist, and in a more cheerful mood Trask went to Grey's house.

"I've done a little digging on my own," the old man told him, after the detective had taken a seat and refused a drink. "I noticed in your dossiers that all the Ashcroft sons went to Wordsworth Academy near Kernville. It happens that the headmaster there, Martin Sandys, was a classmate of mine in college. He gave me some confidential data on the three of them. It's not to be spread around, but we can at least draw some inferences from it.

"To begin with, two of the boys had normal, if undistinguished records there. But Harry Ashcroft is an interesting case. He was not only mischievous and ingenious—note that last—but was really hipped on the family record and the chivalry idea in general. He organized and was president of the Chandos Club, which promoted a lot of knightly and medieval customs.

"But Harry wasn't basically a chivalrous sort. He forced a duel on another student, and they actually used unbaited foils—very dangerous. It was believed that Harry tried to run the other boy through, but was lucky enough to get only his arm, and the matter was hushed up. He also had a nice taste in revenge, especially on his inferiors, as he saw them, or the underbred. He pulled a particularly nasty trick of that kind on a poor refugee, a Dr. Komarewski. The details don't matter."

Trask was looking a little dazed by this spate of information, and Grey added quickly, "But that's enough on Harry for the moment. Let me get to another point. It seems that about twenty years ago Edward Ashcroft had a brochure about the family privately printed. Copies are scarce, but Edgar found one at the U.C.L.A. Library.

"The brochure contains a few things of interest, remembering that the old man hammered away at his kids. The motto of the first Ashcroft, Harold, knighted in 1148, was *Caveat Actor*—which means *Let the doer beware*. Then, when a later Ashcroft married Alithe de Coucy, he took over her family creed, which involved the figure of a badger in the coat of arms and the words *I bite hard*."

The lieutenant shifted impatiently, wishing Grey would get to the point. It wasn't like the old man to ramble this way. Trask didn't realize that Grey needed a sounding board to test the validity of his converging suspicions.

"Now, one more point. Sir Kenelm Ashcroft, in 1525, was thought to be in league with the Devil. At least, when his enemy, Count Dewhurst, attacked Ashcroft's castle, a freak storm came up, and the lightning knocked the count out of his saddle; it killed three of his men too. After that, the Ashcrofts used to say, *My vengeance is a thunderbolt*.

"They're fighters, dirty if necessary, and vengeful, if history means anything. I'm not talking nonsense about heredity or throwbacks, but only stressing what young Harry may have picked up, what may have made an indelible impression on his mind.

"There was an Ashcroft who knew Abraham Lincoln—or so the pamphlet says—and the account claims that Lincoln said of this one: 'Rafe is the kind of fightin' fool who'll grab a wildcat by the tail 'thout ever thinkin' of the consequences.' Then he added, 'But when it's over, old Rafe'll have more tail than the cat will.' "

"I get the general idea," the lieutenant said diffidently. "But we were pretty sure one of the Ashcrofts did it."

"The frame fits Harry best," Grey said. "That's the main point. Now, what I'd like is to have Edgar look around the roof of the Pelletier Building. He may need you to get him up there, past the custodian or manager or whoever handles such things."

"The Pelletier Building! But, good Lord, that's so far away—and higher. You can't be thinking—"

"I'm told," the scientist cut in, "that unlike Ashcroft's place, it's open late—dance studios, rehearsal rooms, and such facilities. And there's an electric sign on the roof," he added meaningly.

"But it must be a hundred and fifty feet away. You can't electrocute anybody at that distance—except with a science-fiction death ray!"

"Edgar checked the City Engineer's maps. It's exactly one hundred and five feet, horizontally, and three stories, or another forty-six feet, vertically. I computed the distance from one edge of the Pelletier roof to the swimming pool on the Ashcroft Building as a hundred and thirty-nine feet."

"What's Edgar looking for there?" the lieutenant asked, seeming slightly dazed.

"I'm not sure," was the evasive reply. "You needn't actually go in person. Send a man—or call the superintendent; that would do."

"Not on your life!" Trask said. "Whatever Edgar's searching for, I want to see, too."

"Can you meet him there about two?"

"You bet. I'll be in the lobby."

"Then we're set. If I'm lucky in my guess—and it's pretty wild—you may get the break you need."

"And how I need it! The D.A.'s on my back like an army knapsack loaded with rocks."

"There are two things that a theory of this crime must account for," Grey said, following the detective to the door in his wheelchair. "The wound in Baker's shoulder, and the significant fact that all the men were in the pool. I would say the killer had to have a good observation post to take advantage of that. He might have to wait an hour or more without being watched or questioned."

Trask blinked.

"I hadn't thought about that last point. And you think," he said, "that Edgar will find the answer on the Pelletier roof?"

"We'll know later," the old man said calmly.

"Still claiming to be only fourteen, you dwarf?" Trask greeted Edgar in the lobby.

"Nope," was the quick retort. "I was fourteen-and-a-half last week, so now I call myself fifteen."

On the roof the boy sauntered about in an exasperating way, but finally closed in on the leads to the big electric sign. It was a quick and fruitful search. There was a cut in the BX cable, exposing the wire-pair inside, from which some insulation had been stripped. The whole job was clearly a recent one.

Edgar took out a small camera, attached a close-up lens, and photographed the cut in the cable.

"I think that's all," he said, "but no harm in looking around for a bit."

"By all means," the lieutenant said ironically.

But after a brief examination of the parapet nearest the Ashcroft Building, Edgar professed himself satisfied, and they left. When they parted in front of the building, Edgar said, "You'll be hearing from Dad soon, I think. He was right, as usual."

Although he shouldn't have been surprised, Trask was. His jaw dropped.

The next morning Grey sent for him, and the detective broke all speed records getting there in a police car.

"You saw the BX cable," the scientist said, as soon as Trask strode in. "They have two hundred and fifty volts up there—not that the usual one hundred and ten wouldn't do."

"All right," the lieutenant said. "The current's there, but how did it get to the pool nearly a hundred and fifty feet away?"

Grey held out a length of pale wire.

"This is modern lamp-cord stuff. It has the usual pair of copper braids under insulation, but is super-light. A hundred-foot coil weighs only two ounces plus. The hundred and thirty-nine feet the killer needed wouldn't come to more than three ounces. Yet it can carry a normal load for an appliance."

Trask gaped at him. "But how could he get it over to the other building so far away?"

"When Harry Ashcroft ran the Chandos Club, he gave an entertainment once. His part was demonstrating the crossbow, and for a kid of fifteen, he was very good."

The detective sucked in his breath.

"Holy jumping—! You mean he *shot* the line across?"

"A heavy war-bolt would do it if the wire was coiled to avoid snarling. Remember, too, he was shooting down. And I suppose he practiced a bit first—to get the ballistics of dragging such a line through the air. But he could hardly miss something as big as a swimming pool.

"I figure he cut the BX with a hacksaw, attached one end of the wire, and bared the copper strands at the other end, keeping them from touching, naturally. I would guess, too, that he prevented a short circuit against the iron bolt by using a few inches of string to fasten them together.

"All right, then. The bolt flies off, tugging the bare leads by that short length of non-conductor, and pulling loops from the main coil as it goes through the air. He had a perfect spot to shoot from: the Pelletier Building is busy until late at night; there's a lot of noise— singers and pianists practicing, dancers tapping, orchestras going full blast, and people lugging instruments in cases. He could carry a wrapped crossbow, and never be noticed.

"It was dark on the roof, except near the sign; but the swimming pool glowed as a fine target—one he could hardly miss. Nor could anybody on the street or on another building see what he was doing. The bolt and wire would sail down from one dimly lit roof to another, far above the ground. Anywhere in the water would do. And if he missed, he could simply try again."

"That wound!" Trask exclaimed. "He hit Baker!"

"Exactly—he must have. But not intentionally, I would say. In fact, it must have been a bad moment for him. He had to free the bolt by pulling on that light wire, and if it had snapped—trouble! The evidence left in plain sight by the pool.

"But luckily for him the gash was shallow; the bolt wouldn't have much velocity, dragging all that weight. He hit Baker while the fellow was climbing in or out; no doubt Harry Ashcroft had to wait until everybody was in the pool. He wanted them all, and no witnesses, either. Anyhow, the hot leads touched the water and killed all the poor devils instantly."

"And you think Harry's the one."

"By far the most probable suspect. Remember his nature—vindictive. And his ingenuity at school. Not to mention his being so full of that medieval stuff about his family and their glorious past. An Ashcroft had been treacherously injured—swindled out of his rightful heritage and paralyzed. *Caveat Actor*, but in the plural: *Let all the doers beware; I bite hard.* As to proof—"

"That's always a problem," the lieutenant said.

"He may have been foolish enough to put that crossbow back in the house, where he almost certainly got it. And the bolt—you could test that for blood and tissue. You might even turn up a hacksaw blade there with filings in the teeth to match that BX cable spectroscopically. Also, question all the people in the Pelletier Building that night; when those wires hit the pool, the lights in the Pelletier Building should have flickered or fuses blown.

"And I don't think Harry will let his brothers be implicated, if it comes to a pinch. Assuming you do find evidence in the Ashcroft house, they'll all be under suspicion, and my guess is he won't want that—he'll confess. Not that you need it; he's the only crossbow expert in the bunch."

"It's a fantastic explanation," Trask said. "I wouldn't buy it from another soul. But I know you—and it really fits the facts. Nothing else does." Then, somberly: "I'm glad Harry's not married. The hell of all crimes is that so many innocent people—on both sides—get hurt."

"I wonder," Grey said slowly, "if Harry ever thought about that other motto. An iron missile, carrying a deadly electrical charge—certainly he avenged the Ashcrofts with a thunderbolt."

The Scientist and the Invisible Safe

There were times when Lieutenant Trask wondered if he put too much faith in pure logic. Not that he was naive enough to expect criminals to behave like mathematical elements: he knew that many people were wildly improbable in their actions, and that crooks were often the wildest. But the facts, at least, should make a coherent pattern, with no inconsistencies or contradictions.

He was more hurt than angry when he emphasized this point to Cyriack Skinner Grey, who sat in his wheelchair listening. Grey would always sit there, having been paralyzed in a mountaineering accident. But there was nothing wrong with his brain, which was that of a well-trained research scientist, and holder of an enormous amount of data, all available for instant reference. And if Grey's brain wasn't quite up to an extraordinary demand, it could be supplemented by a library of thousands of technical books. And for a legman he always had his brilliant fourteen-year-old son, Edgar, with a high I.Q. and low laugh-point.

"In a way," the scientist told Trask in his mellow baritone, suggestive of a bronze gong, "you're rather ungrateful to a kindly universe. Most of your cases are both irrational and illogical. That is, Joe Doakes, having consumed six or eight fluid ounces of methyl alcohol, decides that Bill Brown has insulted the great garden state of West Carolina, and brains him with an empty fifth.

"There are nine eyewitnesses; the man's fingerprints are on the bottle; he even confesses, and weeps over his sin. After which, probably, a jury convicts him of involuntary manslaughter, and an Appeals Court frees him over a flyspeck mistaken for a comma.

"Now, tell the truth: can there be much creative enjoyment for you in handling such a matter? So you really should be delighted with any problem that offers an intellectual challenge. Or am I talking nonsense?"

"I don't say that," Trask admitted, though not very enthusiastic about the reasoning. "But I've got a diamond worth a quarter of a million dollars hidden in a hotel room—just a few square feet of space, and not exactly cluttered—and I simply cannot find the blasted thing! The D.A.'s screaming like a blistered eagle; the owner, Countess Elena Braganza, a V.I.P. from Brazil, is chiming in with not very ladylike wails of her own. And the thief, Doc Meinecke, is laughing his head off at all of us. That kind of challenge," he added sourly, "I can do without."

"And your complaint against logic, I take it, is that since a room has only X cubic inches of space, what one man conceals there, another should be able to find—right?"

"Exactly."

The scientist pressed a button on the arm of his chair, was offered a thin, very black cigar by a humidor that swiveled out invitingly, and lit it at a disk that glowed red-hot nearby. For the detective he filled a fragile cup, translucent and pearly, from a tiny spigot; it might have been bourbon he drew, but it was black coffee, steaming hot. Trask nodded his thanks, and sipped the fragrant brew greedily. It was some kind of sea captain's coffee, strong enough to yell like Tarzan, but never bitter.

"Sounds quite intriguing," Grey said, blowing three quick smoke rings. "Let's have the details."

"This Doc Meinecke," Trask began, hitching his chair closer to the scientist's, "is the cleverest jewel thief in the business. The old—ah—fellow always uses the same *modus operandi*, and why not, since it's never failed him. He gets his paws on a prize gem—second-story stuff, con game, sometimes even a stickup; he couldn't care less. Then he takes a hotel room. Pays for two weeks in advance, so that if he's arrested nobody else can move in—not that they'd find anything; *we* can't. He wants the same room available after making bail, which he gets every time, hiring the best lawyer around. Not that he's held in most cases; Doc seldom gives any grounds for arrest—he's too slick an operator.

"Well, once settled in the hotel room, he waits for buyers, having sent out word about the merchandise. The top fences show up and bid. Most of the details are straightforward, but Doc has one gimmick all his own. He claims to have a private little invisible safe to carry the loot in, and to hide it safely in the room. I tell you, Professor, cops all over this country, and in Europe, too, have caught him in a hotel room absolutely sure a valuable jewel was hidden there, and have never once found it.

"Doc gets a bang out of that record. He brags about his 'invisible safe,' and even gives the 'combination': P 6-2-3. Only nobody but Doc knows what it means."

Grey hunched deeper in his wheelchair, his deep-set eyes shining like embers.

"And," the scientist said softly, "now it's your turn, eh? You've trapped him in a hotel room, but you can't find the Braganza diamond."

"Right. We got a tip and took him by surprise. Well, not really. He always has a few minutes' warning somehow—enough to put the loot in his hiding place. But we know the stone's still there—it has to be— in fact, Meinecke makes no bones about it. He was chortling like crazy all the way to the precinct house. The old buzzard knows we can't hold him more than forty-eight hours at the most. Then he'll go back to the room, and wait for us to give up the search.

"Sure, we can stake out the hotel, but a fox like that can smell a cop. He won't make a move until he's sure we've gone; we haven't the men or budget to watch one crook for long. But if we could only find that diamond before Meinecke gets out of jail, then it's his finish. Not to mention getting the D.A. and the Countess off our backs."

"A very interesting problem," Grey said. His eyes grew blank with thought. "The logic is quite clear. Obviously his hiding place must be something not only normal for any hotel room, but a location utterly above suspicion—invisible, not literally, but one the police see right through, and don't dream of checking. There can't be many such hiding places in an ordinary hotel room—in fact, offhand, I can't think of even one. But we're bound to spot it in time."

"That's the trouble," Trask said bitterly, "we don't have time. Believe me, we took that room apart. There's a definite routine; nothing is missed. Furniture, floor, walls, fixtures, electrical outlets, plumbing, strings dangling out of windows, goo against outer walls, ventilators, ducts, ice or food in refrigerator, if there is one. We've even broken eggs, so help me. You can soften part of a shell, insert something, and patch it up so it looks new. The diamond *can't* be in that blasted room—but I'm sure it *is*!"

"And the combination, you say, is P 6-2-3 … hmm," the scientist said.

He sat immobile, not even blinking. His amazing brain, like a huge computer hunting chess moves, worked with great speed and precision. Trask guessed what he was doing. Grey was undoubtedly visualizing a typical hotel room, and then inventorying it one cubic foot at a time. Like the tormented genius, Tesla, the professor could call up anything ever seen—and some concepts never before seen—in full color and in three-dimensional detail.

Trask watched him quietly for ten minutes, his own body so tense that the muscles began to ache. Then Grey sighed, blinked, and a wintry smile touched his lips.

"I may have it," he said. "At least, there's only one hiding place that seems to qualify. But let me see if the combination Doc gave is consistent with it in some way. P 6-2-3. Tell me, what do you know about Doc Meinecke's background?"

"Well, he's not a real doctor, of course. That's just a title his fellow crooks gave him for having a bit of education."

"College?"

"Yes and no. He started out, believe it or not, in a theological seminary."

Grey cocked his massive head.

"P 6-2-3. Now, I wonder … hah! Bible, almost certainly. But which part. P for proverbs? VI—um—two-three. Don't recall." He flipped a switch on the left arm of his chair, and Edgar's voice came over the speaker on the wall.

"Yes, Dad."

"Bring me a Bible, will you, son?"

"Right away," the boy said, and shortly appeared with a bulky volume.

"Hi, you fifty-year-old dwarf genius," Trask said. "Still claim to be only fourteen?"

"I'm ready for you this time," was the grinning reply. The redhead held out a document and a big sheet of film. "My birth certificate—and an x-ray showing sutures that establish age."

Grey smiled, and Trask gulped.

The scientist took the Bible, riffled the pages, and said, "Not two-three. Let's try twenty-three … well, now." He looked at the lieutenant. "Did you happen to notice a light in the room that seemed rather dim for its size?"

"A light? No, I didn't see—wait a minute! You trying to tell me that—"

"I certainly am. A light bulb—on and glowing—is the only explanation that makes sense. Nobody ever would suspect it. After all, it's shining; it's brittle glass; it must have a vacuum, and it won't function if it's broken. How could a lit electric bulb possibly hide anything?"

"That's what I'd like to know," Trask said fervently.

"What Doc did, I'd say, is use the heavily frosted bulb of a high wattage light. It's easy enough to break off the brass end—a little flame would do it, properly used. Then he could fit a *smaller* bulb inside, with a tight friction joint where the metal part of the smaller bulb sticks out of the hole at the base of the larger bulb. Or if he's not handy himself, some friend with a glass cutter and a few simple tools could rig the thing.

"Now, when you screw the 'double' bulb into a socket, you'd be connecting the smaller bulb, which would glow inside the outer empty-glass shell. Since the outer one's frosted, nothing inside would show except the light. Probably to make sure nothing showed he'd fill the extra space with some non-inflammable packing—say, glass wool. So even if somebody unscrewed the bulb—"

"Which I did to every bulb in the place to check the sockets!" Trask moaned. "What an idiot I am. And I remember now that Doc had a sleeve of new bulbs and an extension cord. Camouflage, of course, so that when the trick bulb was being transported from home to hotel we wouldn't spot it; lots of people bring their own light bulbs to hotel rooms. Brother, was I fooled!"

The lieutenant jumped up, anxious to get back to the hotel room. Then he paused. "Almost forgot. What about that combination?"

Grey lifted the Bible.

"The particular proverb goes: 'The commandment is a lamp; and the law is *light*.' A bit vague perhaps, but close enough to justify Doc's little joke."

"It may be his joke," Trask said, "but we'll have the last laugh—thanks to you."

He grabbed Edgar's x-ray, studied it, and said, "Only fourteen, you say? How come I see a small metal plate in the brain that reads '1920' and underneath—why I can hardly believe it!—'Made in Japan.' "

"Go find your old diamond," the boy grinned; and the detective did just that.

The Scientist and the Two Thieves

"What I can't understand is how you cops keep losing stuff. Now it's a fortune in diamonds—in a blind alley, too. Tsk!"

The speaker was Edgar Grey, who had a normal fourteen-year-old, run-of-the-mill body—Model Naked Ape, Junior—but a space-age brain that sparked an I.Q. of 180, often rising higher under forced draft. He also had a somewhat mordant sense of humor better suited to George Bernard Shaw at ninety.

This time, however, his comment was entirely without malice; he liked Lieutenant Trask. The feeling was mutual, but in the detective's case it was spiced with a soupçon of awe. The mental machinery behind that freckled young face could be disconcerting on occasion.

Cyriack Skinner Grey, the boy's father, a scientist and a sometime crime consultant, took in the scene with benign amusement.

"A hit—a palpable hit," he said. "Edgar has a point. You chased the robber into a cul-de-sac, presumably with his loot. The only entrance was then blocked; there was no way out, yet the stones vanished. I remember Wilde's quip that to lose one parent may be regarded as a misfortune, but to lose both smacks of carelessness."

Trask grinned. "It is rather funny in the abstract," he admitted. "But fifty thousand dollars' worth of property has been stolen, and that's serious. Worst of it is that Lou Burgin's not even a criminal type; more of a religious nut. He robbed, I suspect, only to finance his new 'Stand Tall for Christ' movement. You should see his room—full of tracts, collections of musty sermons, garish photos, medals, crosses, icons, you name it—and a dozen Bibles, some fancy and illustrated. There's a Doré that made Cliff Garrett lick his chops—he's a book-collector. But Burgin reads while eating—even Doré—and isn't very dainty, so when Cliff saw the inner pages, wow! I was afraid we'd be booking him on Murder One!"

Grey pressed a button in one arm of his wheelchair; there was a hissing sound, and the smell of coffee, expertly brewed, filled the room. A tiny ceramic cup rose from a recess. Grey handed it to Trask, who sipped the Kona—the scientist's private blend—with appreciation.

"Suppose you start from the beginning," Grey said. "As I understand it, Burgin caught the manager about closing time, forced him to open the safe, and then made off with a packet of diamonds. And he used a gun."

"Right," the lieutenant said. "But I doubt he'd have fired it. Anyhow, when Kelly, the off-duty detective, happened to see him running from the place, he gave chase. Burgin panicked and got trapped in that blind alley. He threw the gun away while running, but must have wiped it clean—even the dumbest amateurs know that much these days.

"Well, no officer is supposed to go after a felon alone; Burgin might have had another gun for all Kelly knew. So he followed the book and waited at the head of the alley, knowing the robber couldn't get away. But, as I've said, when the cruiser came with help, and the men advanced, Burgin gave up without a fight—only there were no diamonds."

"Did he drop them on the way?" Grey asked.

"Almost impossible. Kelly was right behind him and it was a short run along open walks. Anyway, we searched the route immediately and found nothing."

"But you did mention the light was bad; it was about dusk."

"True, but the one block he ran was well-lit, and Kelly is certain he didn't dump anything—not before entering the alley. And if the loot is in there, we sure can't find the stuff."

"With no prints on the gun, and no diamonds, you don't have much of a case against Burgin," Edgar said. It was not meant as a jibe; his tone was sympathetic.

"That's right. But getting the diamonds back is more important," Trask said. He drank the last of the coffee, smiled wryly, and added, "There's even beginner's luck in the crime. This clown made a heist any pro would envy, but he picked the Ace Jewelers at random, knows almost nothing about gems, and got this packet because the manager was scared spitless—afraid of guns—and Burgin's old .45 may be too corroded to fire!"

"Don't blame the manager a bit," the scientist said. "Any sane person should be afraid of a .45." He touched the cigar button, received two Havanas, and tossed one to Trask. "What's the alley like?"

"One side is a big apartment building; the other's the old State Theater—abandoned, boarded up; just a housing project now for pigeons, sparrows, even a few crows. It was dark in the alley, none of the tenants saw a thing. The diamonds aren't hidden anywhere—that I'll swear."

"The roofs? Could he have thrown them up on one?"

Trask shook his head. "A top outfielder might make the roof of the theater, but Burgin's a weedy little guy. Not one man in a hundred could do it."

"What was the weight of the package?"

"About four ounces. A small sack, actually, made of soft leather, I believe."

"Good for throwing," Grey pointed out.

"I agree. But where to? The apartment is six stories, and State Theater a bit lower, about five."

"I can't say you're wrong; that's quite a throw," the scientist admitted. "Well, suppose you give me the data and photos. I'll read through the material and try to figure some angle. And I'll pick Edgar's brain, too; he's beginning to stagnate lately!"

"Good idea," Trask said gravely. "Give his peers a chance to catch up."

74

"At least he's starting to enjoy poetry as well as math," Grey said. "Yesterday he was quoting *The Jackdaw of Rheims*—ever read the *Ingoldsby Legends*? Quite good light verse; much better than most of the genre we see today."

"If Ogden Nash wrote 'em, yes; otherwise, no," the detective said, grinning. "See you later—I hope," and he left.

It was a comparatively thin file that Grey studied. The case was almost too simple. The tenants had little to contribute; details of the search were useless as generators of good ideas. After ninety minutes the scientist put down the folder and sighed. Only one tiny implication worth investigating. He maneuvered the powered wheelchair to a phone and called Trask.

"I don't really have a damned thing," he said right off. "But I'm mildly intrigued by the overturned trash can."

"We didn't find any diamonds there," Trask assured him.

"That's clear enough from your data. But would it be too much trouble to have the tenants inspect the contents and tell you if anything is missing?" Then he added in an anxious voice, "You've sealed off the area, of course."

"You bet. Until we rule out that the stuff is there someplace. I can't imagine," he went on, "why anything taken from the trash means much—if Burgin dumped the can—but knowing you, I'll get the information immediately."

"Fine," Grey said. "Let me know if anybody misses anything he or she threw out."

"I'll do that," Trask promised, and hung up.

Late in the afternoon Trask called back. "Only thing I have," he said, "is what one woman told us. There was fancy paper from a gift in the trash, but the string, a colored, flashy tinsel type, was gone." He paused, then asked, "That suggest anything to you?"

"Not so fast," was the plaintive reply. "Give me time to think— meaning right now I've not the foggiest idea it means a blooming thing. Why should it?"

"That's your bag," Trask said. "Plausible inferences."

"I'll set the inferencer to work, but promise nothing. String, eh? I wonder. Call you back if something surfaces." He hung up, and with something like a sigh, opened the folder again.

Two hours later he rang up Trask. "Wild idea," he said, "but plausible in a way. Biblical scholar, string—does that suggest anything?"

"Not to me. Should it?"

"What if Burgin got ingenious? Been reading about David. Dumped that trash can looking for a cord; found the string, tied it to the sack—"

"By gad!" the detective breathed. "A sling! With that he could make one of the roofs. If you whirl a stone hard and fast—I've done it as a kid—it really carries."

"It's certainly a possibility," Grey said. "And the only one I can offer you. So try the roofs."

The expected call from Trask came the next morning. The lieutenant sounded very subdued, almost embarrassed. "I'm sorry," he said. "Nothing on either roof. I really thought you had the solution, too."

There was a pregnant silence, then Grey said, "Odd. Nothing? Hmm … I was beginning to feel rather sure …" He laughed. "Just as well, maybe. I shouldn't expect to score every time. Not that I'll give up, so, back to the old drawing board. What's left? Not on the roof—imagine that!"

After hanging up Grey sat unmoving, a faint frown on his face. He saw in his theater of the mind an intriguing drama. The frantic thief, trapped in the blind alley, his hasty rummaging of the trash can, the finding of a string—then Burgin whirling the little sack faster and faster, angling it more to the vertical—and the calculated release, with the bag and comet tail of glittery cord soaring to a rooftop … and then—and then the screen went blank …

Now he turned to the photos. The State Theater roof was more likely; the apartment house was really too high even for a sling. All right, what was up there? Again the screen glowed … pigeons, not his pet birds—flying rats, they were called, and rightly—dirty, not very birdlike compared to robins, jays, jackdaws … *Jackdaws … Rheims …* and the light came …

"Binoculars?" Trask asked in a bewildered tone. "Sure we have 'em—good 7 by 50's. What do I look for, and where?"

"I must warn you," Grey said, "it's a long shot—longest shot since the 75-mile Paris gun."

"Your long shot is better than point-blank with some, so fire away."

"All right. You scrutinize the trees, the taller ones, on all sides of the two buildings. What you're looking for is that flashy string with, I devoutly hope, the sack of diamonds still attached. And no questions, please; my neck is already out ten miles. Just search, and if you find them—"

"You'll hear about it," the lieutenant said, and tactfully added not another word.

Later, at a triumphal conclave, Grey explained in detail. "I was almost certain that Burgin did use a sling; why else would a string be missing from the trash? Kids nowadays have too many toys to collect things the way we did in my generation. But after landing on the roof of the theater the diamonds must have disappeared again if I were right. Yet the building was boarded up, the roof quite inaccessible—except to birds. Then I happened to think of Edgar and the jackdaw from *Ingoldsby*. You," he looked at Trask, "did mention a few crows on the roof. Odd, by the way, how in recent years they've taken to urban areas. When I was a boy you rarely saw one even in a small town, much less a city; but with farms dying out—well, no matter. Point is they love bright objects. What member of the Corvidae could resist that glittering piece of string? He'd surely take it to his nest or perching place. Four or five ounces is no burden for a big crow. So it was a double theft—first Burgin, then a greedy bird!"

"I had to get a snorkel from the fire department," the detective said. "The sack was up in a tall tree; luckily, as you thought, the flashy cord made it easy to spot with binoculars. After only a dozen trees, too—might have been fifty. How far can a crow fly?"

"Quite a ways," Grey said. "But it was reasonable that a bird using the State Theater roof had its perch close by."

"The Jackdaw of Rheims," Edgar said, "stole a bishop's ring and was cursed with all the power of the church; it plumb near ruint him!"

"Not that the bishop hated birds," the scientist added. "That clerical broadside was against the 'thief'—he had no notion, until later, that a jackdaw had swiped his episcopal ring."

"By the way," Edgar asked, grinning, "when do you pick up the guilty crow and book him for grand theft, jewelry or whatever?"

Trask's mouth twitched. "First off, you disguised midget," he said, "there was no felony committed; merely failure to report finding stolen merchandise—a misdemeanor. Secondly, you have my word that if somebody can pick the thief out from among six other crows at the lineup, he'll be charged!"

The lieutenant stalked off, much elated. It was not often that he had the last word with Edgar.

The Scientist and the Time Bomb

Lying well back in his wheelchair, Cyriack Skinner Grey carefully read the most unusual letter of his career. It was addressed not to him, but to the governor of the state, and Lieutenant Trask, who had just handed it to the scientist, now waited anxiously for his reaction. Perhaps he expected a hint, at least, of amusement, even derision, but Grey was obviously not responding to a foolish hoax. An odd message, to be sure, but with a tone that implied neither a practical joke nor a fantastic, paranoid threat. The writer seemed deadly earnest, and the personality behind the typed words did not suggest a disturbed mind.

The letter went as follows:

To the Governor and Legislature:

Gentlemen—

This is a warning from beyond the grave. My lawyers, who are unaware of these contents and have no share in my actions, were directed to mail this letter fifteen years after my death, which is due within weeks, as I am seventy-two years old and have terminal cancer.

This year the covenant made by the state with my grandfather, Jeremiah Coleman, is being immorally, if not illegally, broken, and his historic house, full of valuable and lovely things, is no longer free to the public. In complete disregard of its solemnly pledged word, this government is about to hand the estate over to a private company that will charge admission; there is even the possibility that the house will become the governor's official residence, barred to the public except on special occasions. Therefore, from across the Styx, I am now going to destroy totally the Coleman Mansion I love. Within a few months, at most, it will be blown apart, and it is your responsibility to clear the grounds at once, and thus save lives. There is nothing you can do to prevent the explosion.

(Signed) Horace Coleman

Grey looked up, a tiny fire blazing in each eye, to meet Trask's inquiring gaze. "Remarkable," the scientist said. It was a word he didn't use lightly.

"Is it possible?" the detective asked. "A bomb with a fifteen-year fuse? Nobody could have planted one undetected in the house since Horace Coleman died. The place has been open to the public daily, guarded at night; tons of priceless stuff in it; fantastic collection, really. A small San Simeon, and well-patronized."

"Offhand I'd say no. But I don't give such hasty opinions to be taken seriously," Grey added with a smile. "You've searched, I'm sure."

"Right. Inside *and* out; there's a lot of thick shrubbery."

"Did Horace have any dedicated, fanatical heirs who might agree with him about a government swindle?"

"None close enough to be affected. The arrangement was that after Jeremiah died the property passed to the state, the only qualification being that his son Micah and grandson Horace live there for life, with no rent or property tax, but allowing the public in free daily. When Horace died fifteen years ago, there were no more Colemans eligible to move in, and the state ran the house as a free museum. But before that, in the sneaky way the letter mentions, the legislature reneged and decided to honor the contract only fifteen more years. So now, with Horace long gone, the new plan takes effect and the people pay admission. Dirty, but quite legal; they found a loophole of some kind. Probably, too, the taxpayers were unhappy; aren't they always? Anyhow, that's why Horace was burned up and planned this revenge: to destroy the house about the time it goes private. But getting back to that offhand opinion—"

"Just from the top of my head, then," Grey said. "Batteries won't last; they leak, corrode. There are some that keep until started by puncture or particular activation procedures, but that only pushes the problem back a step; what energizes the activator? Acid works quickly or not at all. To have a wire eaten away and release a spring-loaded detonator, how do you open a vial of acid after all that time? A spring-loaded plunger to break the glass—but what releases the spring and what keeps it from rusting away? There's air pressure and temperature. You could count on a high in either in X years, and set a spring detonator to react, but why is X fifteen, and how could anybody guarantee that the barometer or thermometer wouldn't go high enough tomorrow or next week?"

Trask gulped, almost gaping. Grey must work like a giant computer testing for primes, trying hundreds each second.

"You have ideas—possible solutions—I couldn't think of in years," he said. "But you throw them all away."

"Premature, anyway," the scientist said. "I need to know a lot more about friend Horace. What kind of a man was he? Where and how educated, for example. Hobbies, special expertise; you see the point."

"Of course. Well, he was a Harvard graduate and very brilliant. Majored in science, but turned later to biology; invertebrates were his field, which must mean more to you than me. For thirty years, until his death, he was a professor of biology at Hayes Technical College. Lived in the family home-museum, as I've said, but had very little income except from his job; grandfather lived it up while still here and didn't leave much except the house to his heirs. And that only to sleep in, you might say; the state held title; nothing could be sold. One of the Fragonard paintings would have set Horace up, but it seems he wasn't bitter; loved his teaching and was good at it."

Grey jabbed twice at a stud in one arm of the chair, and two cigars rolled out of a recess into his hand. He tossed one to Trask, and lit his own at a disc that suddenly glowed red near the button.

"Ah," the lieutenant said, "Havana—you smuggler!"

"Not at all," was the bland reply. "I have a Cuban refugee friend who brought out ten thousand of the best, well before our ill-advised quarantine. But back to our moutons. You see, Trask, my ideas won't work—not with the kind of certainty Coleman needs—or needed; hard to remember he's fifteen years dead. But he was filled with a strong grievance, and had quite a while to ponder the matter, so we can't really rule out such a fuse, however improbable it may seem." He puffed furiously for a few moments, then said, "You could take him seriously enough to clean out the house—remove all the art objects."

"Only up to a point," the detective said. "Much of the best stuff is permanent—part of the building. Molded cornices, tiles, archways, stained-glass windows, gorgeous hardwood floors—no end to it. We could save the Renoirs, El Grecos, and such."

"I see. Well, we can't let such a collection get blown up. Give me your data on Coleman and I'll go over them today."

"Got it all right here," Trask said, opening his briefcase. He handed Grey a large, fat envelope.

"This could take some time for even a faint glimmer," the scientist said. "At the moment, I've not an inkling. A fifteen-year fuse, even eighty percent reliable—golly! You've no idea what that implies. Although," he added, "there's silica gel—keeps things dry, unrusted."

"*I* don't have any answers," the detective said smugly. "But you will have; the governor expects it."

"Damn the old mugwump," Grey snapped. "My sympathies are with the Colemans; but this official had no part in the deal. Now clear out of here and let me hallucinate. A fifteen-year time bomb—oh, brother!"

Grinning, the detective left.

Patiently, with his customary thoroughness, the scientist went through the thick dossier. "Began with classics, I see," he muttered. "Hence that crack about the Styx. Then general zoology, and finally the invertebrates … arthropods … better check his publications … never can tell … *Respiration in Periplaneta Americana*—there's a fascinating topic!"

He read steadily for two hours, then took up the photos of the house. They were big glossies, microscopically sharp. The crime lab had a Hasselblad and knew how to use it. Quite a place, all right; baroque but impressive … dense shrubbery, particularly along the south wall … decades old, he'd estimate …

Finally he was finished with the dossier. He pressed a button in the arm of his chair, and a crystal flask of brandy rose up and out of a recess. He sipped it very slowly, thinking hard. The germ of an idea was hovering tantalizingly at the edge of his brain. Suddenly he went rigid, then laughed. Absurd! It was incredible, nonsensical, and yet …

He flipped a switch, and the chair, propelled by an electric motor, went smoothly up the ramp to his second-floor library, which housed over five thousand books. With the aid of a long rod that ended in padded tongs, he took down volumes by Fabre, Essig, Lutz, and Imms. He leafed through these eagerly, pausing to scrutinize certain passages. Fabre, that incomparable observer—stylist, too—had it all. But Grey wasn't quite convinced; simply too wild.

He maneuvered his chair to the phone, and questioning his own sanity, put through a call to Harvard. Brian Foote, an old friend on the faculty, was his target. After an exchange of greetings, Grey got to the point.

"Brian," he said, "I'd like you to get me the title of a Ph.D. thesis and maybe a Master's, if any. The name is Horace Coleman; he graduated with a doctorate in zoology in 1922. Could you get me that information right now?"

"Why not?" Foote said. "It takes only a call to the librarian."

Twenty minutes later Grey had the answer, and his eyes widened. The crazy inference—none too plausible—had paid off. Surely this was the heart of Coleman's plan, spectacularly ingenious even with a hint from Nature's own timing and a very useful coincidence. But what about the bones and muscles, the implementing anatomy? He went into deep thought again. Something incorruptible was needed. Nylon monofilament, say … maybe gold wire; why not? … a heavily-greased sleeve into the big box … takes plenty of dynamite, gelignite, plastique, or whatever, to pulverize a large building from the outside … In his mind's eye he could now see the whole mechanism, and Grey was consumed with admiration; tomorrow a consultation with the Lieutenant …

Trask arrived early; in fact, had he dared, the detective would have turned up at sunrise. He sat on the edge of the chair and almost groaned with impatience as Grey drew him a cup of black Kona from the recess in his automated chair.

"Relax," the scientist said. "I'm almost afraid to give you my suggestion, it's so wild. More of a guess than a probable inference this time—but it does add up."

The detective sipped the superb coffee and waited. It was Grey's show.

"What you'll need to do," the scientist said, "is probe all the ground around the house—" Here Trask groaned. "—but only up to about ten feet away and twenty or thirty inches deep. You'll be looking for a rather large box, perhaps several feet square. Move the earth away carefully, in small amounts, and be sure to cut any and all threads connected to it."

"What kind of threads?"

"I don't know, but something durable obviously, if they've lasted fifteen years in damp soil. Nylon, gold—something of that sort."

"I don't understand any of this," Trask said. "Tell me before I go nuts."

Grey held up a small bottle full of clear liquid. Inside was a leggy corpse which the detective immediately put in the category: bug, large and messy.

"This," the scientist said, "is the larva of the periodical cicada, also known as the 17-year locust. It's your patient bomber."

Trask seemed unable to speak, but his lips moved soundlessly.

"I'll explain. Imagine a big box full of explosive with a detonator—no, two, for insurance—operated by a small but steady pull on a straight wire of stiff metal. Running into the box, through well-greased sleeves—or one bigger opening, say—very thin, strong threads or wires. These," he said slowly, watching the detective, "would be attached to several larvae of the cicada, carefully, so as not to injure them or even keep them from feeding. Threaded through the chitinous top of the thorax, I'd guess. Now," he added in a brisk tone, "Coleman puts box and larvae deep into the ground among thick shrubbery, on which the insects will feed happily for the fifteen years left of their cycle—they were two years into it, clearly, when he got them. They are not inclined to move—so says Fabre—with plenty of food around. All right. After fifteen years, meaning months from now, they move up to carry out their metamorphosis. Insects, you must know, are enormously strong for their size; some can move, even lift, ten or more times their own weight. You've seen ants go at it. Well, with a dozen of these pulling on their threads, all attached through one hole, or several, to the detonator complex in the box, it's damn near certain the light, oiled metal pin will be dragged loose. That releases the spring, and boom! Scratch one house. Coleman, by the way, did his doctoral thesis on periodical cicadas."

"Joe's dead and Sal's a widder!" Trask muttered, totally unaware of dredging up, after forty years, a favorite cry of wonder used by a maternal aunt, long since dead. "I know you mean it, but—"

"So far, still only a plausible inference—pedantese for reckless guess—but probe anyway; then we'll see."

Three days later the word came. Trask was exultant. "Almost exactly what you predicted," he said. "Big box of dynamite, thirty-two inches underground, and at least eight of the bugs, fat and sassy, with long, thin tethers. Actually they could roam quite a bit without pulling the pins—two of those, each with a detonating spring. Silica gel in the bomb; even greased tubes for the wires. You'll be glad to know," he added, "we didn't kill the cicadas; just cut 'em loose—with a warning!"

Grey chuckled. "You said 'almost' right. Where did I slip?"

"It was platinum wire, but very fine; the lab boys think Horace must have drawn it out from the regular gauge."

"I should have thought of that," the scientist said ruefully. "Common in chemistry classes; gold isn't."

"Too bad about you," Trask said. "Only 99 percent on the beam!"

He came by a month later, carrying a flat parcel.

"The state can't legally give you a Coleman Fragonard," he said, "but Mutual of Maine can buy one, and at my hint, since you saved them about five million bucks in insurance, they did so. I hope you like it. You'd better; not many Fragonards on the open market, so little choice. But it looks good to me."

For once, Cyriack Skinner Grey was speechless.

The Scientist and the Platinum Chain

"I hear they're changing the name of your department to *Lost and Found*. Is that true?"

Edgar Grey's freckled face wore an expression of sweet and honest curiosity. It was a friendly jibe, if somewhat short on tact, but Lieutenant Trask didn't strike back; instead, he rolled with the punch, slyly turning the other cheek.

"You're batting five hundred," he said. "We're the 'Lost' part; you two handle 'Found.' "

Cyriack Skinner Grey, relaxed in his wheelchair, smiled at the exchange, mentally calling it a draw.

"First a sack of diamonds, and now a platinum chain," Edgar said. "What next?"

"You, I hope!" the detective said. "And I won't even ask your father to help in the search, because there won't be any!"

"Platinum's a very heavy metal," the elder Grey said, snubbing both of them. "A chain of over a hundred links, even small ovals, could weigh five pounds or more."

"A good estimate," Trask said, a note of admiration in his voice. "They told me sixty-two troy ounces—they run twelve to a pound, as I'm sure you know—or about eighty-three ordinary ones."

Edgar whistled softly. "That's what's disappeared this time? And in a locked room, yet—to coin a phrase." He was only fourteen, but had an I.Q. high enough to justify a "genius" rating, and the chutzpah of the ten most feisty cabdrivers in New York. That he was amiable and good-hearted may be credited to paternal guidance and example, particularly the latter. "Must be worth a fortune; what's platinum selling for these days, Dad?"

"Last time I bought some—a crucible for the lab—it came to one hundred sixty dollars an ounce, as a rough estimate. It's scarcer than gold and a lot more useful."

"The chain's a mere ten-thousand-dollar item," the lieutenant said. "But that's not the problem; the company probably spends that much on paper clips annually. It's almost certainly the murder weapon, which is what bugs us. The victim was strangled—garroted, so to speak—with something like that, judging from the marks on his neck. And," he added, looking at Edgar, "the room wasn't locked."

"I didn't mean that literally," the boy explained. "It's just a term used in detective stories—which you guys never read, any more than doctors go for medical fiction—for all cases where the victim apparently couldn't have been killed in the circumstances. That is—" Here he broke off in some embarrassment.

"A good definition will take more thought," his father said dryly.

"Nevertheless, I get his point," Trask said. "And he's right. There's no way that chain could have disappeared, but it did."

He saw Grey jabbing at a shiny metal box on one side of the wheelchair, and asked, "Say, what's that? New, isn't it?"

The scientist-engineer, having lost the use of his legs, spent much time in the chair and, as his friends maintained, not altogether in jest, had fitted it with more conveniences than many a luxury apartment.

"Yes," he said. "It's a cooler, much miniaturized, with no bulky compressor; uses the thermal-electric cooling effect that was developed recently. Now I can offer you iced tea, lemonade, or even ice cream. Not you, Edgar," he added with mock sternness. "You can make it to our refrigerator, and this thing holds only about a quart." He looked at the detective. "What'll you have?"

"Lemonade will be fine," Trask said, fascinated as he watched the golden liquid spurt fragrantly from a tiny faucet into the glass Grey held under it. He sipped, nodded approval, and said, "It's really cold; your gadget works," and as Grey's eyebrows rose, added quickly, "as I'd expect."

"So far," the scientist said, "we've had just a few highlights. Now let's have it from the beginning; seems an interesting case."

"Right," Trask said, gulping the last of his drink. "The murder took place at Ezekiel Cooper & Sons; a very old firm, started over a century ago, and still run by the family. Silversmiths, although nowadays they also work in gold, platinum, and even rarer stuff for alloys; maximum security, naturally. With all that gold around, especially at today's prices, nobody gets out unsearched to the skin." He handed the empty glass to Grey, who refilled it.

"The man killed was Noah Cooper—they go for biblical names—new president of the firm. His father, Esau, died a month ago. Well, Noah was in his suite of rooms, busy with lead soldiers …"

Here he paused, obviously expecting a reaction, which was immediately forthcoming, but from Edgar, who exclaimed, "Wha-at?"

"That's right," the detective said, smiling a bit wryly. "With all that gold around, Noah Cooper went for molding lead soldiers—and don't sneer; he duplicates rare old types that sell for fantastic amounts. Even his modern replicas cost plenty, and they're meticulously made for accuracy and detail; beautiful work. Anyhow, he has the little lab as part of his suite. He melts the lead over a gas flame, by the way. None of that is relevant, probably. What counts is that he was a mean and nasty fellow, very hard to get along with by anyone's standards.

"Now, the suspect: old employee named George Witherspoon. He's also a hardhead, but a real artist in metal. Best man they have, but set in his ways and full of pride. Hates to take orders, which Noah likes to give, unpleasantly. Naturally, they clashed the minute Cooper took over from the former head, his father. Wednesday last, Witherspoon was hauled up on the carpet again; Noah wanted him to cut corners on a fancy gold medallion they were making for a wealthy industrialist, and the old man balked. Admittedly, he's slowed down a bit, and is crotchety, but does do top work and won't be rushed. People outside heard them quarreling, then a scuffle of some kind, but didn't dare go in; Cooper didn't welcome anybody meddling or even coming in unless asked. OK, about ten minutes later Witherspoon comes out, looking rather dazed, and says, 'He's dead.' I should say," Trask went on, "that while Cooper was only thirty, and the old man sixty-two, anybody could spot the winner if they tangled: a flabby hundred and twenty pounds against a hulking, vigorous two hundred; in fact, the old guy could have pinched Noah's head off with two fingers. But the fact is, or so it seems, he used the chain." He paused for a long drink of the cool lemonade, cleared his throat, and said, "The chain; in 1900, when the firm was already well-established, Jacob Cooper had the idea of a company chain, one platinum link for each year since their founding. Everybody went for it, so today there are a hundred and twelve links and the chain hangs from two sterling hooks in the president's suite—or did; now it's gone."

"Simple," Edgar said. "Witherspoon melted it down after the murder."

"Not over a gas flame, all Cooper has in there," the lieutenant said quickly. "None of the fancy ovens and torches used in the real workshops. I looked into that, sonny; platinum melts at seventeen fifty-five centigrade. Just try getting anywhere near that with gas!"

Grey nodded approval. "Absolutely right," he said.

"Nor did he toss it out of a window," the detective said. "There aren't any, as such; the whole building's sealed and air-conditioned. Partly for dust control, but also in case of theft. No, it wasn't dropped to the street, nor down the john, either; we checked—although a long, five-pound chain doesn't go down a pipe very handily—beyond recovery. Witherspoon didn't take it from the office; too bulky to hide in his clothes, and plenty of people saw him come out."

"But he did report the death," the scientist said. "How did he explain it?"

"He didn't. Maybe it was shock at first, but having refused to comment, he now says, in effect, 'I didn't do it, because if I did, where's the chain?' As to who else could have done it, he denies that's his problem. He's a rough old boy, quintessential down-Easterner in some ways."

"It must be hidden in his offices," Edgar said confidently. "No other possibility, is there?"

"So it seems," Trask admitted, "but we can't find it. We even re-melted Cooper's caldron of lead—he was making soldiers when Witherspoon showed up, it appears—thinking he might have dropped the chain in there. Since lead melts at only three twenty-seven degrees, the platinum would just be imbedded in the mass when it hardened. But no dice; not a scrap of platinum in the stuff when we poured it out. And of course we ransacked the suite, too. There's only the one door, where Witherspoon came out in full view of six office-workers, so—" He shook his head, lips pursed. "And don't tell me," he admonished Edgar, whose mouth was opening, "that he made all that platinum into fake 'lead' soldiers in ten minutes—and over a piddling gas flame. They're all lead. Idiotic as it seems, I even checked that—I don't know why. When a soldier weighs like lead, is soft like lead, shines like lead, melts like lead, then it's lead—period!" He looked at the elder Grey for confirmation.

The scientist was laughing, a full-throated, joyous sound, as he said, "I'd say you're right about the soldiers; the time element alone would rule them out." Then he said cryptically, his deep-set eyes twinkling, "There was a time when a dentist would take off his gold ring before going to work." Trask and his son both looked at him, their faces equally blank. "Ed, please go upstairs and get me the big chemical encyclopedia. You know where it is." It was characteristic of their relationship that he said please.

The boy gave him a wondering glance, and left.

"Tell me," Grey asked the lieutenant, "did you get the impression at any time that Witherspoon himself was puzzled by your failure to find the chain?"

Trask hesitated, thinking. "Now that you mention it, his reaction was a bit odd when he heard some details of our search. But, damn it, he must know where the thing is; he put it there!"

Edgar returned with the huge reference book, and handed it to his father.

"Excuse me while I check an old man's doubtful memory," he said with outrageous hyperbole, since his memory included even the logs of the first hundred integers. When he looked up from the book a few minutes later, there was a tiny fire burning in each eye, different in kind and intensity from the previous twinkle.

"About the dentist—" Trask began, but was interrupted.

"The old-timers made their own fillings by mixing silver and mercury to get amalgam. Now, mercury swallows up gold as easily as silver, although it's a noble metal and resists most reagents except aqua regia, a mixture of nitric and hydrochloric acids."

"No acids or mercury in Cooper's rooms," Trask said.

"Not the point," Grey said. "There was molten lead, and as I just verified—it's not well known even among people like Witherspoon working in precious metals exclusively—platinum does dissolve in lead. You didn't find a whole chain in the lead mass, but I'll bet you have a mighty valuable alloy in that caldron!"

Edgar and Trask looked at each other wordlessly.

"I didn't ask *you*," the scientist told his son, "because you specialize in pine beetles and math. Maybe now you'll learn a bit of chemistry!"

When the detective called back the next morning, he reported verifying an iron pot full of lead-platinum alloy—and a confession from Witherspoon, who was charged with manslaughter, having killed in an angry quarrel, and not in cold blood. In a panic, he had dropped the chain into the melted lead, thinking only of immediate concealment, and never dreaming it could be undiscovered for long. Which prompted Edgar to tease his father with the remark: "So there are times when it's better *not* to know chemistry!"

The Scientist and the Exterminator

El Supremo, Luis Alvarez Ybarra, was dead, and Lieutenant Trask, who bore little of the onus for the general's sudden demise, mourned him not as a fellow human—few would be that compassionate—but purely as symbolic of an embarrassing blunder. The deceased was also known as "The Butcher of Corona Del Norte," which accounts for many dry eyes in his native land.

Most of the black marks in the unfortunate matter went to the FBI, with a few demerits left for the State Department, since it was mainly the business of these two well-funded organizations to protect foreign dignitaries.

"Don't quote me," the detective said blandly. "A good cop isn't supposed to condone homicide, and I've never done it before. Or hardly ever," he added, being an honest man. "But the extermination of Ybarra hardly strikes me as a terrible crime. He was a mass-murderer himself, and worse, a torturer who loved his work. But I do hate not knowing just how it was done, which is why I'm here bothering you again."

Cyriack Skinner Grey, settling deeper into his wheelchair, smiled. "I can understand your feelings," he said, cocking his massive head in a typically quizzical way. "An exceptionally intriguing case, judging from the newspaper accounts."

Trask hesitated, then said rather diffidently, "What picture did you get from their stories over the last few days? Mind telling me?"

"Not at all—why should I? It'll save you from rehashing the whole thing." He pressed a button on the arm of the chair, obtained a small mug of coffee, and handed it to his guest. It was a special blend of Kona, dark and heavy. For himself, he pushed something the detective couldn't see, and came up with a small, greenish apple. "Like 'em tart," he said, taking a bite. "I'd better do it chronologically, so I can organize my thoughts and remember all the significant points. To begin with, Ybarra was supposed to stay for a week, and came for an operation, not at all dangerous, but very tricky. His hearing was failing, and we have a surgeon who specializes in correcting the calcification of the tiny bones involved. It's such delicate work he uses a microscope and minuscule implements.

"He was given a room in the Grant Hotel with top security. That meant the rooms above, below, and on all sides were kept vacant. There were guards in the corridors watching his door and the others, too—the ones for empty rooms.

"Outside, the hotel was also closely guarded on four sides, day and night. Finally, there was a man on the roof at all times.

"Nevertheless, on the night before his move to the hospital, somebody managed to introduce a large amount of cyanide gas into the room. Ybarra was in bed, asleep apparently, and didn't know what killed him. Some would say," Grey added in a hard voice, "he got off too easy. But there it is: a room nine floors up, with six more over it, maximum security in every conceivable way, yet he was killed."

"You have the facts right," Trask said. "But there's just a bit more. We even have the empty gas cylinder; it was found in a trash can two blocks from the hotel. And to top that, we know where the killer operated from—a room in another hotel across the street—but it's almost fifty feet away, although at about the same height as Ybarra's. But how he got a cylinder weighing ten pounds across from his window to the Hotel Grant one ..." Here the lieutenant shook his head in wonder.

"Did you also find out where he got the gas?"

"That was easy. A pest-control outfit was burglarized some days ago. Good choice; maybe the only one. Not many places keep cyanide around. 'Bug-Out Exterminators'—there's a name for you!"

"How did you identify the killer's room?" Grey asked, dropping his apple core into a slot.

"Routine matter. We checked everybody who rented a room there since Ybarra came. Of several possibles, only one looked like a Latin American, and in his room, which he took by the way, as 'James Carillo'—not his real name, of course—we found clippings about Ybarra, left there, I think, just to taunt us. Why he didn't leave the gas container, too, I don't know; but neither did he try very hard to dispose of it effectively; wanted us to find that as well. One of your political, radical-idealist types, no doubt; proud of the murder."

"How was the gas introduced?"

"Nobody knows," Trask admitted. "I didn't get to see the room right away. You know the FBI; they look down on cops. Well, they think it was either the ventilator or the air-conditioner—what the hell else could it be, with a guard at the door?—but don't really know which, if either. I forgot to mention that to prevent a sniper from the hotel across the street, there were not only heavy draperies inside Ybarra's window, but a chicken-wire cover outside, just in case somebody tried to toss a grenade or bomb in—on the ninth floor, mind you! What from, a helicopter? To install it they had to use a sort of window-cleaner's scaffold setup."

"Did it also cover the air-conditioner you mentioned? It was a window type, wasn't it?"

"Yes. Tricky business. Had to have a bulge to go over the intake part, which sticks out about eight inches."

"In a way," the scientist said, "security helped do Ybarra in. I understand that the guard at his door smelled bitter almonds and knocked, but naturally the locks were all set and he couldn't get in until much too late."

"That's true, but if he had got in we might have two bodies; the room was loaded, we're told. The FBI people backed well off to let the air clear. Bad stuff, cyanide gas."

"Well," Grey said, "the facts so far are simply not adequate for a highly probable inference. I need more data."

"Like what?" Trask asked eagerly.

"Did you check the air-conditioner thoroughly?"

"The FBI did, and found nothing of interest. They had hoped to find some kind of time-delay canister inside, I suspect; that would have cleared up the matter—to a point. Anyhow, I looked it over when they finally condescended to permit it. Didn't find anything."

"It doesn't take much," the scientist said. "Suppose you could bring me the filter?"

"Probably. Although it was pretty dirty; should have been changed long ago. But the Grant Hotel is starting to cut corners; maybe too much modern competition. Newer places, for example, have central air-conditioning. Do you have an idea?" he added wistfully.

"Not really, but something in the filter might suggest one."

"Then I'll bring it, even if the room's rented now. As I said, a change is in order, anyhow."

"While you're at it," Grey said, "take a good look at the outside screen."

Trask blinked. "What for?"

"I'm not sure. Maybe a dent; but it could be just a spot where the paint, if any, is chipped." He raised an admonitory hand, smiling. "No use asking questions; I'm just 'hunting,' as they say, about a feedback setup trying to stabilize. I'll say this much: I suspect the gas came in by the air-conditioner, but it's only a hunch or quasi-reasonable guess based on the Holmes axiom—you know the one—other possibilities too impossible, so the highly-improbable is favored!"

The detective looked at him wordlessly. "I can't even comment sensibly on that," he said in a plaintive voice. "I'll be back with the filter and a reconditioned brain, obviously needed around here!" and he stalked out.

Moments later, rather sheepishly, he returned. "Forgot to give you the file—what there is. Not very much, and little you don't already know; but the photos may help."

"Good," Grey said. "I'll go through it."

The scientist studied the material in a way oddly desultory for him; his mind seemed to be elsewhere. Actually, he was convinced circumstances were so limiting that a solution ought to suggest itself even at this point, assuming one had enough imagination. From one room to another, fifty feet away, both about ninety feet high—that was the crux of the puzzle, even with no additional data. But a heavy cylinder—ten pounds Trask had said—across such a gap and without elaborate or massive equipment, no way …

He examined the photos. Only one seemed to interest him; it showed that the area between the two hotels was actually a small park; that could be significant. Late at night, when the murder was accomplished, few, if any, people would be around. It also implied a degree of darkness; the killer could do—well, whatever he did—those nine stories up with little chance of being observed; in fact, his entire operation might be totally invisible from so far below in such circumstances. Noise, of course, was another matter. How could he get the gas cylinder across in relative silence?

Dead stop. He pressed a button in the arm of his chair, and when the little crystal goblet of old brandy proffered itself, raised it to his lips even as they twitched briefly. Cure your delusions of infallibility! he admonished himself. James Carillo is too clever for yours truly. Smiling, he sipped, savoring the excellent liquor. Then it was back to the dossier, and the baffling puzzle that had produced it … But after two more hours he was still without answers. Sighing, he gave up the riddle for that day.

The filter, once Grey had a chance to examine it, proved a familiar type, consisting of glass wool supported by a rectangular frame. It was quite dirty, but not clogged, so on that warm night—Ybarra's last—the general would have had no reason to fiddle with the cooler.

The wool was mostly dark grey, but city air can do that in hours. There were, however, scattered patches of black. It was in one of these that Grey found something of interest. He picked at it with tweezers; a shred of black, shiny stuff, nearly invisible in the soiled fibers of the filter. The scientist studied it with growing excitement. The theater of his mind, with imagination as the seasoned producer, came to life.

Damn the gas tank; its weight was no longer an obstacle to a convincing theory; now it was only a matter of journeyman work, mere implementation of the basic concept, a brilliant one, Grey thought, with admiration.

When Trask came back for a briefing, the scientist made no attempt to conceal his elation. He held up the scrap of material, and said, "Here's what fooled us. It's polyethylene, the stuff they make weather balloons from. Carillo didn't need to transport a heavy cylinder across to Ybarra's room—just a balloon full of gas!"

The lieutenant blinked, then smiled approval, but his reaction seemed subdued.

"That makes a difference," he admitted, "but still, getting anything across there is more than I can figure out."

"I won't say it was done this way," Grey said, "but here's how it could be accomplished—how I'd do it.

"Start with a small, powerful magnet, alnico type; weight about an ounce. Fasten a short wire around it with the free end having a loop, to serve as a pulley. Now take a hundred feet of fishing line, monofilament, light and strong, say two-pound test weight, and pass one end through the wire loop. With the two free ends at his window, Carillo projects the magnet against the wire mesh near—just above, he'd hope—the air-conditioner."

"Wait a minute," Trask interrupted. "What do you mean 'project'? How?"

"Can't say for sure. One way would be a good modern slingshot. Or with a dowel fastened to the magnet, you could use an air rifle. There are many ways. Probably we'll never know which was used. But, to go on, Carillo now has a sort of endless clothesline running to Ybarra's window, once he ties his two ends together. All right; he fills the balloon with cyanide gas from the cylinder—very carefully, I'd assume!—ties it to the filament, and by pulling on the line moves the balloon over to the general's window. There he pops it; the released gas is sucked into the cooler's grille, and that's the end of Ybarra."

"Slow down," the lieutenant pleaded. "How does he pop the balloon?"

"Same answer," was the airy reply. "He could have used the slingshot, firing a ball bearing. Or the air gun with a BB or .22 pellet. Easy, compared to sending the magnet and line across. I suggest," he added, "a search, probably futile, for the evidence."

"Which will be?" Trask asked in a dry voice.

"After the balloon collapses, Carillo would naturally pull on the fishing line. But the chunk of polyethylene, minus the fragment I found in the filter, was bound to jam at the magnet; too bulky for any loop. So that end would fall down to the park. He could easily reel the magnet and empty balloon up to his window, but that might attract somebody's notice, and why should he bother? If he didn't, they should be still somewhere in the brush. By the way, did you check the wire mesh?"

"Yes," the detective said, eyes twinkling. "There was a mark or slight dent, all right. Made by the magnet, I suppose."

"I'd say so. Must have made quite a thump to go all that way carrying a double line; but with Ybarra asleep and not hearing well to begin with … Otherwise, he might have investigated and still be alive."

"It's a wonder nobody saw anything, what with a big balloon moving across from one window to another."

"Little chance of that. It was the middle of the night, dark, an empty park, other guests probably sleeping; and ninety feet up, remember. Besides, the balloon was black; he used some kind of paint or dye; didn't miss a trick, Mr. Carillo!"

"I'll have the park area searched," Trask said.

So it was that some hours later he returned with a crumpled mass of polyethylene to which was still attached a magnet and six inches of monofilament line.

"Evidently got snagged in the shrubbery," the detective said. "Carillo either couldn't find it in the dark or didn't bother, as you suggested. Hauled in what broke loose, I suppose, and took off like a big-bottomed bird. Our hope of identifying him, much less finding him, is nil."

"I'm not too sad about that, are you?" Grey asked, smiling. "Considering his means—cyanide gas—and the character of Ybarra, you might think of it as a kind of amateur, free-lance job of pest extermination."

"Unofficially," Trask said, "I agree. Officially, no comment."

The Scientist and the Missing Pistol

Cyriack Skinner Grey spent much of his physical life in a wheelchair, but mentally he was unbounded. He delighted in probable inferences drawn from factual data, had immense expertise in science and a free-ranging imagination more typical of a poet.

Right now he pressed a stud in one arm of his chair and nearby there was a faint hissing, a melodic gurgle, and the fragrance of fine coffee, carefully brewed. It was black, mellow, and strong enough to deck Giant Despair in round one.

Lieutenant Trask, smiling his thanks, took the tiny ceramic mug, and sipped eagerly. He was tired and rather depressed, as any dedicated cop would be when somebody seemed likely to get away with murder.

"Now," Grey said, "what's the problem?"

It was amazing, Trask reflected, not for the first time, how this scientist, once a top electronics engineer and all-around guru of the physical world and its laws, had made the transition to informal, usually unpaid, crime consultant. He wondered if the city fathers would ever realize how lucky they were to have a man like Grey on tap. And how vitally the man functioned, even from a wheelchair.

Grey had drawn from another recess in his chair, designed by himself with an eye both to efficiency and sybaritic indulgence, a crystal flask of brandy which he tasted with obvious relish, watching the detective a bit quizzically. Being on duty, Trask, he knew, would prefer to skip alcohol.

"Right up your alley," Trask said. "A 'locked room' case, so help me. Guy shot dead in an office with only one other man there—and no gun to be found."

"Ah," Grey said, brightening unashamedly. To him killing was bad, but once done it couldn't be prevented, and while murder was deplorable, a homicide—a less emotional word!—was good; it stretched the mind and helped one forget his useless legs.

"Who shot whom?" Grey asked. "And with what?"

"I suspect," the lieutenant said, typically cautious, emphasizing the verb, "that Steve Duggan killed his business partner, Keven McCallum. But there's no proof at all. As to the gun, that could have been a pistol or a rifle."

"Caliber?"

"A .22 firing a Long Rifle, which, as you know, is a much underrated little slug. Deadly at short range, and can carry well over a mile. Went deep into McCallum's skull from far enough away to leave no powder burns—but that doesn't need more than a few feet, so Duggan certainly could have done it there in the office."

"Why couldn't he have gotten rid of the gun?"

"Well," Trask said slowly, organizing his thoughts, "there's just the one door to their private office. Outside is a bigger room, full of typists, clerks, errand-boys, about thirty busy people. The firm, *Space-Age Plastics*, I should say, does about four million dollars' or more worth of business annually.

"According to Duggan, what happened was this. McCallum told him he was into the Mob for over $80,000 in gambling debts, and that they'd kill him if he didn't pay up soon. Then he admitted tapping the till for about $50,000 of that. Like Duggan, he's a good accountant and business expert, and had access to the books, of course.

"Anyhow, they agreed the best thing was for McCallum to write it all out, sort of confession, then call the police in for protection. He'd have to resign, but Duggan offered to let the fifty thousand go for now, and not prosecute.

"So McCallum sat down at his desk to begin, when suddenly he slumped in the chair, shot dead by a bullet through the open window, or so Duggan claims. Seeing McCallum was done for, no pulse or other signs of life, Duggan ran out to the main office yelling for somebody to call the police."

"No phone inside?" Grey demanded.

"Just what I wondered about," the detective said quickly. "Damn right. Who ever heard of two V.I.P.'s without phones, even a row of buttons, in their office? But Duggan was rattled, he says, and didn't think about anything but rushing for help."

"Could happen," the scientist admitted. "People do crazy things, as we both know. Could he have slipped the gun to somebody in the main office, or taken it out of the building himself?"

"Absolutely not. Too many people were watching him in the big room, and he never left that until long after the police came and everybody was searched and questioned."

"What about the open window you mentioned?"

"Seemed the only solution at first, but below is Hartmann Plaza, and it was crawling with people then. Lunchtime, you see. All over, lying on the grass, feeding pigeons, eating from bags. You couldn't drop an empty cartridge down there and not have somebody spot it falling."

"Why do you reject Duggan's explanation—the bullet through the window? You must have a reason."

"I do. First of all, they had been quarreling for months. Duggan wanted to sell to a big outfit, but McCallum wouldn't have it. And both would have to agree. Then there's McCallum's wife. She says he didn't act like a guy in trouble with the Mob or deep in debt. Sure, people have kept such things from wives before, but Duggan did have a motive."

"What about the embezzlement part; did that prove out?"

"You bet." Trask frowned. "But, again, what if Duggan was the thief? If he could eliminate his partner, sell the firm for a big profit, and at the same time cover his own stealing—"

"If you're right," the scientist said slowly, "he staked a lot on losing that pistol. It couldn't have been a rifle," he added, "since that would really be tough to dispose of in a hurry."

"My feeling, too," Trask said. He grinned sheepishly. "You know, I even thought of a case in Laguna Beach some years back, where a guy used a balloon full of hydrogen to carry off a .25 caliber automatic he'd murdered his wife with. But he could count on the balloon going down in the sea, whereas here it would probably land in some solid citizen's yard! Too risky."

"I assume, then," Grey said, a twinkle in his deep-set eyes, "you'd like to have me find a gun in that private office. And after you and a dozen eager experts have taken it apart."

The lieutenant looked around hopefully. "Where's that midget genius you pretend is a fourteen-year-old kid?" he asked, referring to Edgar Grey, the scientist's son, who had an I.Q. of 180, sharp eyes, enormous chutzpa, and little reverence except for Isaac Newton, James Clerk Maxwell, and Charles Darwin. Plus a bit for Dad.

"Off to camp," Grey told him. "You're out of luck there; we're on our own. He'll probably find a new species of insect; he usually does at camp, and tries to get it named after him. Bound to happen before long. But, as I said, it's up to us; no assistant!"

"Well, I did bring a bunch of pictures, the usual big glossies, of the offices, and transcripts of all the important testimony. Maybe if you go over those—"

"Naturally," the scientist said. "But first, I know you're suspicious of Duggan, but you're also competent and must have checked on any buildings from which somebody might have fired into the office."

"That's right, and it's another fuzzy point. A really good marksman with a telescopic sight might have managed it from a high-rise across the plaza, but even at lunchtime the rooms with possible angles were occupied. Simply no way for anybody to have fired from there.

"I can't say it's impossible," he added frankly, "because nothing is 100% airtight, and maybe some one office was vacant for x minutes and some fast operator rushed to a window for a quick shot, but I just say not bloody likely!"

Grey was studying the large photos. He cocked his massive head. "The two planters stand out," he said in a dry voice. "One on each side of the door." He didn't make it a question; there was no need.

"First thing we searched," Trask assured him woodenly. "They're concrete; would take Paul Bunyan to push anything into those roots, believe me. But we probed, as I said."

"Very well," Grey said. "I'll go over all these data, and if I get any ideas you'll hear from me."

"Fine," Trask said. "From you that's almost a guarantee." He smiled.

The scientist raised one eyebrow. "You expect too many miracles," he said. "I'm bound to miss one of these days, so don't call this case solved just yet."

"I won't," the detective said, grinning. "I'll only relax enough to get some sleep. First in three days," he added, yawning cavernously.

"Before you go to that well earned rest," Grey said, "a couple of final questions, although I'm sure of the answers."

"Shoot."

"I assume both rooms were sealed off or guarded once you'd searched everybody."

"Absolutely. If Duggan stashed a gun in either office, it's still there. Except that it isn't; can't be, can it?" Trask asked, almost piteously.

"Even a small .22 is pretty big. Yes," Grey said, suddenly philosophical. "Today when most things you buy fall apart minutes after the warranty expires, it's interesting to note how functional and durable and really well made a good pistol is. What that implies, I won't say—now. Get some sleep," he ordered. "I can see you obviously need it."

"Wilco, over, and out!" Trask said crisply, and left.

Until late that night Grey studied the photos and read the reports. He saw the end of a drapery rod over the window, and thought of a zip-gun. Any hollow tube would serve; even kids made them in slums. And a .22 is the easiest round to handle in such a makeshift. But something to close the breech was needed; surely Trask wouldn't have missed any improvised contraption fitting the rod—if it was even hollow …

He read more reports; testimony, contents of the offices, what was in the wastebaskets. Suddenly his gaze sharpened. What were *those* doing among the papers and empty envelopes?

When he got to his office the next morning at eight, Trask found that Grey had already phoned, asking him to call immediately on arriving. Eagerly the detective complied.

"Got something?" he demanded the instant Grey answered.

"Maybe," was the measured reply. "Tell me, how long was it after the shooting before you made a thorough search of the inner office?"

There was a fairly long pause.

"Well, we had a lot of questions and general conversation first. At least ten hours. After all, I had no reason to doubt Duggan's story about an outside shot. With all the noise from machines in the main room, nobody could be sure of hearing a shot. A .22 isn't very loud."

"What I'd like," the scientist said, "is a comparison of the two planters. Could you have them measured inside and out and then weighed? Without the plants, of course."

"The planters? But why? They're empty, and I probed—" He stopped suddenly. He should know better. Grey didn't make idle suggestions. "I'll have it done immediately," he snapped.

"Do that, and call me back." And Grey hung up.

The return call came two hours later.

"Had trouble finding accurate scales big enough," Trask told him. "But you scored. One is over two pounds heavier and three inches less deep."

"Ah," Grey breathed. "I think, can't promise, mind you, but I think you'll find a pistol under concrete in the heavy one." When the detective didn't say anything, Grey went on. "Duggan probably brought some ready-mix concrete to the office in a small bag; wouldn't need more than a pound or so. He pulled out one of the plants and made a wet layer of the stuff about two inches thick. Takes some time to harden. So he had plenty of time to shoot McCallum and bury the gun in the soft concrete. He could count on its setting pretty well long before you got around to a thorough search. His story of what happened, murder by organized crime, and all the testimony from people in the offices; that was bound to take time. Naturally, when you looked into the planters, what with their inside bottoms damp and soiled from dirt, you didn't suspect—who would?—that the solid base of one was deceptive, and a little too thick. It was quite clever."

"Hang on; it's right here," Trask said. "I'll break it open."

"I was about to suggest that," the scientist said, then grinned, aware that nobody was listening now.

Ten minutes later Trask came back on the phone. "Bull's eye!" he said. "A .22 Cobra, big as life. Even other shells in it—in case one wasn't enough, I suppose. How the devil did you guess?"

"It wasn't all that chancy," Grey said rather brusquely. "It was those plant clippings in the wastebasket. Why would somebody like Duggan, important and busy, be trimming a decorative shrub all of a sudden?

"Then I realized he'd do just that if one was noticeably taller than the other. Somebody might spot it, and wonder. The raised bottom, you see. So he had to prune the top of the plant down just enough to even the two up again. Which meant the gun probably had to be in the concrete—right?"

"If you say so," Trask admitted in a hollow voice. A querulous note emerged; he was still exhausted. "But how did you figure it? I mean, see things the rest of us look past, or around—?"

"Don't blame yourself," Grey told him gently. "Most of me's immobile, so my eyes and imagination have to do more. By the way, Edgar called, quite excited—for him. He did discover a new insect—a kind of pine wood engraver beetle unknown before. So there may yet be a *Pityogenes Greyii* in the catalogs!" And well pleased with his probable inferences, Cyriack Skinner Grey hung up.

The Scientist and the Stolen Rembrandt

"Nobody loves an informer," Lieutenant Trask said. "He's bound to be, by nature, the worst sort of selfish opportunist, living with or near criminals and selling them for cash. I always feel dirty dealing with one, but no police department—at least, in a big-city, high-crime area—could do very well without them. There are administrative problems, too. He has to be paid for useful tips, and budgets don't allow for that, openly. That means understood lies and outright book juggling, with the commissioner turning a blind eye."

Cyriack Skinner Grey, erect in his wheelchair, may have thought Trask too one-sided; it troubled his orderly mind, which stressed balance in everything. Darwin, he thought wryly, made a point of writing down every objection to Natural Selection the moment it came to his attention, realizing, well before Freud, that it was just such evidence one tended to forget immediately.

"Yet he must have a kind of courage to mingle with the very men, often desperate and brutal, he betrays," Grey observed.

"That I'll have to give him," was Trask's grudging reply. "But often he has no other way to make a living although, to be fair, it's also possible the very risk involved—walking the tightrope—gives some excitement and direction to a shriveled little life, the sort most of these guys have."

Grey reached toward a button on the arm of his chair, then hesitated. "I was going to offer you coffee," he said, "but it's a warm day, so maybe you'd like something cool."

"What's on tap?"

"Limeade, made from fresh limes."

"Great. I'll take about a gallon."

The scientist turned a tiny faucet on his miniaturized refrigerator, and drew a glass of the icy drink, handing it to Trask, who nodded his thanks.

"Delicious," he said, sipping the green liquid thirstily.

"Now," Grey said, "what about Max Rudolph?"

"He's a top fence, one of the best. Pays a fair price and has never squealed on a client. That's rare, believe me. He's the one, according to the informer, who bought the Rembrandt drawing from the thief, and he's the guy who'll peddle it for heaven knows how much. I understand Rembrandt was a superb draftsman, that his drawings bring as much as most top painters' finished oils or whatever. Here's this newly-discovered preliminary sketch of *The Night Watch*, a famous work, for sale to the highest crooked bidder. It could net Rudolph a million, for all I know. The museum says it's beyond price. You don't just find new Rembrandts anymore."

"Why does a man buy something he can't sell, exhibit, or even admit owning?" Grey wondered aloud. Then, answering his own query: "Only a dedicated collector—a true fanatic. Somebody who'll gloat over it in private."

"That's about it," the detective said. "But there's one funny angle most people don't understand. Rich collectors are dynasty-minded, often from old families. They look ahead a hundred years. By then, all the museum people will be dead and gone—they're peasants with no pedigrees to go on that long. Ditto us cops and insurance adjusters. But their great-great grandchildren will 'discover' a lost Rembrandt and can sell it, if necessary, for X millions by then. Weird, isn't it?"

"To me, yes, but not, obviously, to your illegal buyers."

"Okay," Trask said, giving Grey his empty glass and accepting a refill. "We got the tip. Rudolph is taking the Rembrandt on his boat out to sea a few miles, there to rendezvous with the top bidder." He paused, gave the scientist a wistful glance, and added: "Believe it or not, I didn't know Rembrandt from Da Vinci a few days ago; I've learned a lot fast."

Grey's mouth twitched. "You've certainly done plenty of homework," he assured the lieutenant. "But don't forget you got me that Fragonard from the insurance people, and picked up some background on that job."

"Nothing like this!" Trask said fervently. "However, as soon as we got the tip, I contacted the Coast Guard, and they sailed at once to intercept. Rudolph, who's damned wealthy himself—never convicted once, by the way; smart and lucky—has a great boat with an engine that could drive a liner, so he gave the Coast Guard quite a run for their money. He dodged in and out of fog banks, changing course, and used enough tricks to make Hornblower green with envy; but they have radar, so he didn't get away. They finally made him heave to, boarded his boat, and brought Max back to port, where I was waiting." He gulped the last of the limeade, put the glass on a table, and said, "Now comes the bad part. Up to then we were doing great, the U.S. and I working together like precision machinery. There's absolutely no doubt he had the drawing with him; aside from the tip, why else this trip to sea? It wasn't a good day for fun, I assure you; cold, wet, foggy, choppy waves, lots of bitter wind. Okay, I search the ship, and I'm a pro; I didn't miss anything. But no Rembrandt."

"Dumped at sea for later recovery," Grey suggested.

"Possible—barely—but not probable. For one thing, I'm pretty sure we surprised him. He had no idea he'd be intercepted. Then, too, according to the Coast Guard captain, it would take expert and lucky navigation to drop a small parcel, without a radio marker, in fog at that, and count on recovering it days later; currents, waves, wind, bad bottom—stuff all Greek to me, but clear to sailors. I have to take his word on it. No, I can't help feeling the Rembrandt is still on Rudolph's boat—only I can't find it, which is why I'm here guzzling your limeade."

The scientist seemed a little taken aback, which was atypical. "This doesn't seem to be quite for me," he said. "Obviously, to search a boat from a wheelchair is even more impracticable than trying it on a house. I could send Edgar, but—" He shrugged.

"I didn't make myself clear," Trask said. "Of course, a physical examination of the ship is out of the question; besides, I've done that. No, what occurs to me is more of a 'purloined letter' approach. I'm certainly overlooking some obvious hiding place. Rudolph is a very ingenious and experienced fellow. My guess is that when the Coast Guard got after him, he led them a long chase in order to hide the Rembrandt—and did a mighty fine job of it, apparently."

"So Edgar was wrong," Grey said, his deep-set eyes twinkling. "Some detectives do read detective stories after all; 'purloined letter,' eh?"

The detective grinned. "Edgar, the Miraculous Midget, was right; I don't read 'em. But in my Police Science course at the university, the professor was more literary and made us tackle a few of what he called classics. That was first on the list, and I've never forgotten it. Very clever story."

"You do have a point—about Rudolph and the boat. He may have come up with a far-out solution, one that an ordinary search, even by a pro—" here Trask had the grace to redden, "—might miss. Well, what do you want me to do?"

"This," the lieutenant said crisply, taking up his briefcase. "I've got detailed plans of the boat, and photos—lots of nice, big, glossy ones, inside and out, from all angles. You know my cameraman; he's good. Now, if you were to study these, and use that great imagination of yours ..."

"I'm willing to try," Grey said, "but don't look for any miracles. What fooled you on the ground, the locale, so to speak, is probably too much for me, miles away with plans and pictures."

"Maybe so," Trask admitted. "But considering your track record, it just may happen that Mr. Max Rudolph will meet his match. By the way—odd coincidence—he's a Poe collector himself. Does that openly, but I wouldn't be surprised if he has a few stolen items of his own to gloat over. If there's ever a lost *Tamerlane*, which I'm told is the rarest of all Poe works and the rarest, almost, of anything in print, I'll know who might have it in a locked room!"

"Go away," the scientist said, smiling. "You're full of esoteric information today. I can't listen to all that and concentrate."

"I'm leaving. But work fast, if possible. We can't hold Max or the boat much longer; as it is, my neck is way out. I had to trump up, with help from Captain Haskill—the Coast Guard man—some idiotic charge about not having proper life belts on board or discharging sewage in port, or whatever, even to stop him at sea. Except for his known record, without convictions, alas, Rudolph could probably sue if we don't find that drawing—meaning, if you don't!" Wisely, he didn't wait for a reply, but hurried out.

Grey chuckled, cocked his massive head, and began to study the papers and photos, using a lift-up sort of easel pivoted on one arm of the chair. A boat is a small world of its own, very limited as to space, and the plans showed every cubic inch. The Rembrandt drawing, he learned from the accompanying notes, written in Trask's neat, printlike hand, measured only thirty-six by nineteen inches. What that implied about a hiding place was by no means clear. For one thing, it might be rolled up, thus fitting into a cylindrical opening about three inches in diameter and no more than nineteen inches deep. On the other hand, if kept flat—surely Rudolph would not be vandal enough to fold the priceless thing!—the drawing would need a sizable rectangular, if shallow, spot. No, he wouldn't fold it, except very loosely; a damaged Rembrandt would sell for less. But one couldn't rule out a careful, noncreasing arrangement taking up a rather small square, for example. Altogether, a lot of angles; too many for comfort, Grey mused wryly.

For almost three hours he went over the data, pleased, as always, with their completeness, testifying to Trask's competence and care, but he still had no glimmer of an idea.

Pressing a stud in the right arm of his chair, he got a crystal flask of brandy. Taking minute sips, tiny caresses of the palate, he went into deep thought, but the theater of his mind had nothing to show him; the stage was empty …

Sighing, he put the dossier aside, knowing the importance of a fresh start when a problem proved intractable. The small FM radio behind his head came on; he found a Brandenburg Concerto and relaxed, listening.

Thirty minutes later he tried again, this time using an excellent magnifying glass on photos of the ship. He started with the very bilges and worked up. One blank after another; no hiding place missed by Trask revealed itself to his inner—or outer—eye.

Then the deck, the fittings, the mast—it was hollow probably, but the detective had found no openings whatever, so no Rembrandt inside. His eye moved up the mast; the achromatic triplet lens brought out every minute detail in the sharp photo. At the very top his gaze stayed fixed. He reflected a moment as if in doubt, then riffled among the pictures for another shot of the thing that held his attention; left side, right side. He moved the lens in and out, counting … little fires glowed in his eyes … most odd, unless … a matter once again of the plausible inference … ten minutes later he was on the phone to Trask.

"It was right there!" the detective told him the next morning. "Inside the flag. Who the devil would guess a flag had two thicknesses? They're not made that way."

"Right," Grey agreed. "Rudolph must have done this job himself while ducking and dodging through the fog—as you guessed."

"Sure, I did fine there," Trask said ruefully, "but I missed the flag. What made you pick it?"

"First, it was just a wild thought. Like you, I assumed one layer of cloth, so if he'd just pinned or stapled the drawing to it, anybody could have spotted that, even from the deck. Then I thought of two flags fastened together, and studied both sides. That's what cooked Max's goose. In his haste he didn't realize he'd bungled things. You see, one flag was up-to-date, with fifty stars, but the other side of the same flag, presumably, in a different photo angle, had only forty-eight. That told me I was almost certainly right about a two-ply cloth."

"He sewed them in a hurry, all right. When we lowered Old Glory, it became very obvious." Trask shook his head wonderingly. "It *was* a purloined letter thing in a way, after all, wasn't it?"

"I'd say so," the scientist agreed. "Not many things on a ship are more obvious than a flag whipping in the wind."

"Yes," the detective said, grinning. "And a double flag should be twice as obvious—but only to you!"

The Scientist and the Impassable Gulf

A murder may yet be inevitable, and yet quite unpremeditated. Take Jennings Bryan Latimer, named, ironically enough, after a famous pacifist.

Latimer was a man full of suppressed fury and hate, somebody outwardly timid and meek, completely non-violent externally, but slaying multitudes in his imagination. He was tall and broad, but grossly overweight, with a kind of feminine softness, which may account for his being called, contemptuously, if with occasional pity, "Jennie" by his co-workers. He had disproportionately tiny hands and feet, and his fingers were skilled beyond belief, although few knew it.

Like many mild, over-dominated men he was obsessed with weapons of war, and using those talented hands had filled his basement with superb models, perfectly built to scale, and meticulously finished. There were Roman ballistae, battering rams, arrow-machines, crossbows, and enough cannons to present a whole history of artillery in miniature. The latest, chronologically, was a French 75, but, in general, Latimer ignored armaments created after Appomattox; for modern rockets, missiles, and giant bombs, he felt nothing but scornful revulsion.

Add to this first element of the murder-mix a wife, small, bitterly voluble, her mouth an inhuman weapon that should have been outlawed in the War of the Sexes. She was unhappy, childless, sexually deprived and growing old too fast and growing bitter as fast.

Latimer, in short, was a 250-pound time-bomb, and his wife, Charlene, a sputtering fuse.

Every Sunday it was their habit to arise very early—five, in fact—to beat the traffic, and drive to a remote area of the National Forest. There, in a pleasantly wooded spot by a deep but narrow canyon, each was able to forget, briefly, their endless quarrel.

For Charlene there was a familiar but ever-new landscape to be painted, "Pastoral," she would sigh. "A scene that always looks a bit different depending on the season, the play of light, the cloud-formations." And her own mood she could have added—the most important factor. She was a very poor technician in oils; they always turned out muddy; but her friends, if they knew, said only, "You have a unique style." She was not the kind you offended casually.

Latimer, on the other hand, aside from being an expert model-maker, liked to use his toys, and did so with considerable skill, even making calculations of mass, powder-charge, trajectory, or—when firing his little catapults—even elastic moduli, and all with rule-of-thumb, self-taught math.

"Like Napoleon," he told himself, with a great deal of satisfaction, "and Caesar."

Today he was testing a new coehorn mortar, a 12-pounder in miniature built after one in the Maritime Museum, a place he haunted. It fired a lead ball weighing three ounces, and, like all his artillery models, used black powder.

Across the fifty-foot gap of the little canyon was a large swampy patch, ideal for such tests, since the high-arching missile threw up a gratifying little spurt of muddy water as it fell. Each week Latimer brought some model to fire across the gulch. By arriving so early—before eight—he could be fairly sure no ranger or even a casual hiker was likely to catch him in the harmless but illegal practice.

An additional safeguard of their privacy was the route itself, up a narrow, rutted fire-road, which only a vehicle like their All Terrain "Pakmule" could negotiate.

Even then, there had been times they had to use the powerful winch mounted on the front; by running its steel cable to a tree, they could get out of any hole or muddy ditch.

So today the sun shone brightly; the air was mild and spicy; the little coehorn mortar boomed away, dropping its lead balls exactly where Latimer wanted them to go, flinging up spouts of mud across the canyon.

But this was not to be like other Sundays: the sputtering fuse burned to the powder ...

Charlene's painting was not going well; there a touch of arthritis in her elbow, something that happened oftener nowadays. Time's winged chariot seemed very near, and she was growing old fastened to this gross and sexless man who thought of nothing but his silly toy cannons.

She left the easel, walked over to her husband, and began a typical tirade. The excuse was merely a pretence; any little difference from the past week—and there were many—would have served. Patiently, turning away from his mortar, Latimer pretended to listen, his puffy face assuming a penitent expression almost automatically. Occasionally he voiced a mild "But dear ..." more to prove concern than because he expected any favorable response.

Then suddenly, a new factor was introduced. Furious at his very meekness, just another symbol of his maddening emasculation, she dared the unforgivable. Without any warning Charlene placed her shoe against the mortar, which was only inches from the edge of the canyon, and gave it a vigorous thrust. The model tottered, slid several inches, found a depression in the vegetation, and before Latimer's horrified gaze, it dropped sixty feet into the gulch, tumbling, clattering against stones, and shedding fragments of its carriage on the way. He stared after it, numb with anguish.

There was no way a man of his bulk, clumsy on foot, no matter how nimble the fingers, could get down the precipitous wall to the rocks below where, no doubt, the mortar was shattered anyhow. No way. Dozens of careful hours of skilled work wasted.

Like an irresistible flow of white-hot lava Latimer's terrible inner fury, too long suppressed, overwhelmed him. Aside from Charlene's

117

contemptuous naggings there were the unbearable "Hey Jennies!" at the office, the snickers at his bulging softness of body, his high voice, his timidity. "Enough!" he shouted.

His small fingers were strong; Charlene's neck, though scraggly and tough, was no match for them. She was dead in moments, almost without knowing this was the end, and he aghast, but too late, at the upshot of it all. Horror became a crushing reality. He would be found here with her body; no one else around—a clear case of murder. Then he would have to die in turn, never again to build or fire his beloved miniatures. Trapped; no way out of this, just as no way down after his lovely coehorn mortar at the bottom of the canyon.

For half an hour he crouched there by Charlene's body, head in his hands, thinking of nothing but the death-cell, newly legalized. If only he could call it an accident—but who got strangled unintentionally? Or put the killing on somebody else—anybody: camper, tramp, hapless dropout kid; they had no culverins or Dahlgrens to gloat over; they didn't really savor life at all, or count for anything. But that was impossible, too. Nobody around, and even so, what motive? No, he was boxed in; he was the killer; he must die … not that; it was more a hot-blooded act; not death, but long years in prison; just as bad with no models to make …

He lifted his face, pallid, fleshy, many chinned, and peered across the canyon. Not a soul there, either, even though it was late in the morning. Suppose he made it over, first eliminating all signs of his presence here? Might he not claim he'd fired his coehorn from the other side while Charlene took the car here? He could then insist, and be believed, or not proved a liar, that someone else had killed her.

He'd empty her purse, of course, to make it look like robbery by some wandering tramp. But how could he get across? It was impossible, and if he drove the ATV the several miles to where the canyon leveled out, the tracks would give him away. Then there was the time lost; besides, it was vital to such a plan that the vehicle be found right here.

Latimer groaned, lowering his head again. Then, in a flash, came inspiration, magnificent, fantastic, dazzling—but surely practicable.

Excited, he pulled a notebook from his shirt-pocket along with a ballpoint pen, and fell to figuring …

"I think you'll be the first to agree," Lieutenant Trask said, "that of all the puzzling cases I've brought you this must be the most baffling. A woman strangled and flung down in a marshy area—rather violently, too, judging from bruises on her back where she apparently landed— yet not a single damned footprint around; nothing to show that a living soul was near the spot."

He paused. "The mud itself, I admit, would soon ooze over any prints, but all around it is more solid but moist ground. The killer *had* to be weightless not to leave traces on some side of the marsh. It's absolutely weird—impossible."

"It certainly seems so, as you describe the scene, but we both know better. The laws of this universe are rarely, if ever, suspended."

"You're the one to say that," the detective replied, quite properly, since Cyriack Skinner Grey, his informal, unpaid crime-consultant, was well versed in the basic sciences and had a brilliant imagination to spark this technical background.

Grey sometimes said, not altogether in jest, that he specialized in possible-plausible inferences. Although confined to a wheelchair as the result of an auto crash that had killed his wife, he lived a remarkably full life, not all of it mental, since he was adept at lawn-bowling and was a fair archer, easily drawing a sixty-pound bow with his muscular arms. The chair itself was highly automated and loaded with gadgets, mostly of his own design, and all practical, useful items.

"What if," Trask deadpanned, "that big City Hall in the Sky just passed a new one? Like if a killer rubs himself with—ah—ah I won't say toad-grease; not these days, but diorthopyrochatekinol, he can fly."

Grey's bushy eyebrows rose ever so slightly. "Diortho—what?" he asked mildly.

The detective now looked a bit sheepish. "No such stuff, I think. Just a name we made up years ago in college chem class; it was a kind of a silly joke for months."

"Not a bad try," the scientist said, smiling. "Sounded authentically stuffy. For that you deserve some coffee." He pressed a button on one arm of his chair, and the hot, fragrant brew poured out of a small tin spout into a little ceramic mug.

Trask accepted the drink gratefully; he considered Grey's Kona as the best around, and many connoisseurs would have agreed.

"Any ideas at all—even wild ones?" He asked rather wistfully.

"So soon?" the scientist asked, a touch of irony in his voice. "And with you ruling out the best, in fact the only, suspect?"

"What else can I do?" was Trask's glum reply. "There he was, separated from the body by an impassable gulf, and an hour's drive, at least, by car. He drove to town to report that his wife was missing, and our timetable simply doesn't allow for the trip by road to the other side. He couldn't have done it, period. The killing or the drive. Or crossed the canyon, either. No way."

"A desperate man can do wonders," Grey pointed out. "Or a woman. Like lifting a car from a pinned infant, for example; little women have done just that at times. So admitting Latimer's big and soft, still, if scared enough, mightn't he not have scrambled across somehow, carrying his wife's body? She's a lightweight, you said. Although," he added, "I can't see how he did it without leaving tracks in the damp soil in and around the swampy patch. It's a poser."

"No, it's all out of the question. Aside from his physique and the sheer steepness, you should see the bottom of that gulch; it's solid milk-thistle, the most thorny stuff known to man. Anybody ploughing through that would leave most of his clothes and half his skin. And the jabs of those infernal needles—I can testify, believe me, after poking around down there—would have him howling in agony. No, Latimer didn't go across the canyon, I guarantee."

"Milk-thistle," Grey said. "Yes, I know that lovely weed, and have to agree. You're a very thorough fellow, as I've noted before. You should get combat pay for tangling with milk-thistle!" He looked at one of the papers on his desktop, hinged to the wheelchair. "Purse empty, I see, making it appear"—he emphasized the word slightly—"like robbery."

"Right, but a mugger who leaves no tracks in soft ground … Confound it, Latimer still fits best. They were always quarreling, the neighbors say. If you call it quarreling when she did all the yelling and he just took it. But it must have made him angry, meek a guy as he was.

"You know as well as I how these quiet, repressed types suddenly break loose. It's always some honor student who never says a harsh word to anybody, who obeys and loves his parents to pieces and is admired by everybody, who goes hog-wild without warning and shoots up a dozen innocent people he doesn't even dislike."

"Finish your coffee," Grey said calmly. "You're exhausted. Going at it too hard—you'll never get a useful idea that way. When I find myself blocked and tense, I drop the problem for a while. You go home and take a nap. Let me chew on this for a few hours. Neither of us believes in winged killers, except with feathers, so there has to be a rational explanation."

The detective smiled wanly, finished the coffee, handed the mug over, and prepared to leave.

"I shouldn't get so involved," Trask admitted. "I know better. And, as a matter of fact, I don't burn to nail Latimer. He's only one more inoffensive guy who finally cracked under pressure. He's had a lot to put up with—they call him 'Jennie' where he works, and don't mean it too kindly or in fun. His wife was a real terror, on his back all the time. Not that she didn't have problems," he added, fair-minded as always. "As a husband he was no prizewinner, except that he did provide well and didn't beat her up. Too busy with his cannons to give her the attention any woman needs."

"A fine craftsman," Grey said. "Edgar was enthusiastic over those miniatures you showed him at Latimer's house." Edgar was the scientist's fourteen-year-old son, just like any other healthy boy with genius I.Q. and the self-esteem of a De Gaulle. "And he agrees about the canyon, I might add. Says he wouldn't crash through that growth of milk-thistle without a suit of armor—the complete Fifteenth Century kind!"

"Okay," Trask said. "I'll get out of your way and might even take that advice about sleep. I could use some—about a week's supply." And he left.

Alone, Cyriack Skinner Grey riffled through the dossier again, studying the glossy eight-by-tens taken by the police expert's

Hasselblad. The canyon was clearly a formidable barrier, wide and deep, even aside from the nasty milk-thistle that overgrew the bottom.

There stood the ATV, a sturdy, four-wheel-drive vehicle; it had been photographed back at the scene, across from the body, where Latimer had driven it with the police after reporting his wife's disappearance.

Latimer had explained how they had quarreled, after which Charlene had left on foot, saying she couldn't stand the sight of him a minute longer, and would paint somewhere else for an hour or two. When she had failed to return by noon, Latimer said, he got worried and began a search with the Pakmule. Unable to find her, he then drove to the ranger station and finally to the police in town.

To the surprise of all, when the party came back to the area, there, in plain view across the gulch, was Charlene's body, face up in the swampy patch. Even from far away they could tell she was dead; soldiers and cops know that limp, bundle-of-rags look all too well. Of course, Latimer insisted, she hadn't been there when he left on his search; he'd have seen her, wouldn't he? He wasn't blind.

The group—two police and a ranger—then drove back down, around the end of the canyon, and up another rough road leading to the slough where Charlene's body lay.

The unfortunate woman had been strangled, flung down violently in the mud, and the killer had managed this without leaving a trace of his presence!

There was no possibility that her body, even if weighing only ninety-odd pounds, could have been thrown into the swamp from a dry area, since the nearest was forty-seven feet away. Truly a weird puzzle, Grey reflected, pondering all the data.

He was sipping brandy from a tiny crystal flask, drawn from a tap in the chair's left arm, and admiring photos of Latimer's models—why had Trask included those? Because he was competent and realized no one could tell in advance what evidence was relevant; a scientist manqué, in fact!—when the germ of an idea quickened in his brain.

Immediately, Grey activated his Theater of the Mind, a method of visualizing and coordinating random thought about a case: the scene of the murder as it might have been … Latimer, Grey assumed, strangled her in a rage; no premeditation ... admits she shoved his darling toy into the gulch ... that sparked the quarrel there ... Okay; she's dead, and he's stuck with the corpse ... alone, desperate; didn't intend to kill her ... lost control ... but that won't bring her back to life ... what to do? ... Try to put the crime on somebody else ... anybody, just so it seemed impossible Latimer had done it ... consider all that and the body across the canyon, but no trace of a killer ... and Latimer's hobby ... expertise ...

Grey stiffened in his chair, eyes glowing. Well! More of a highly implausible inference this time. Absurd. Impossible, obviously; not even Paul Bunyan could do it ... and yet it *was* done; stranglers don't fly ... no new Laws of Physics were passed last week. Grey's eyes returned to one of the photos, and just as inspiration had come to Latimer, it touched the scientist ...

When Trask came by two days later, he looked well rested, because the strange case was closed and Latimer—the poor devil—was in jail.

"We found the marks on a sapling, just as you suggested," he told Grey. "One hell of a brilliant idea the guy had."

"It was his specialty, his life, almost," the scientist said. "Old artillery, *including catapults*. Naturally, he'd think of using a tough young tree to flip the body across the canyon. But what stopped me at first, and must have bothered him for a while, too, was how. He's no Hercules, obviously, and not even a pro football linesman could bend such a trunk.

Then I saw the winch on the ATV in a photo, and all was plain. He could winch the sapling down into a perfect catapult, tie it in place with a rope, put the body in the branches on top, and then just cut the rope. With what he knew about such devices he could be pretty sure the corpse would make it across. The slough, which hid the fact of such a flight—hard ground would have done so much damage to her that any coroner would catch on—may have been an extra break he didn't count on or see the need for. But you're right; all things considered, a brilliant notion."

"Well," the detective said. "It wasn't a cold-blooded killing, so he could be out in a few years. He's one more genius who was unlucky enough to meet somebody of the same caliber—mental, not temperamental, I hasten to add—meaning you!"

"Scratch the disclaimer," Grey said somberly. "Any of us is capable of killing, given the right circumstances. Don't even exclude me."

Trask said nothing, but he knew Grey was right.

The Scientist and the Poisoner

Every Thursday evening for the past twenty-three years Hector MacNeil Burrington had been eating dinner in the Tudor Room of the Empire Hotel. In all that time his choice had never once varied: roast leg of lamb, medium, with mint sauce, a big bowl of the finest petits pois, a baked Idaho—plenty of whipped butter—garlic bread, rice pudding, and black coffee. The price, of course, had risen from a modest $2.75 to almost nine ersatz dollars, but the old man didn't gripe. He was a multimillionaire, and unlike so many of the species displayed no perverted stinginess in small matters, paying generously for good service, without either arrogance or condescension. A short, thickset man, he looked rubicund and hearty, very much the pleasant country squire right out of *The Pickwick Papers*.

This time, however, he was enjoying his last solitary feast, because Sunday would mark the end of his long bachelorhood, and also—but this he was not to know except in a brief, agonizing revelation—his murderer was at that moment only a few yards away, preparing to strike.

Midway through the meal Burrington scanned the other diners, vague figures in the dimly-lighted room with its widely-spaced tables; the restaurant still retained its luxurious ambience, how much longer none could say in these days of eat-and-run. He eyed them cheerfully; some knew him casually, and nodded. He swallowed a mouthful of food, stiffened, gasped, and with an incoherent cry, oddly shrill, fell forward, his head, dropping grotesquely, upsetting the bowl of peas, so that they rolled over the cloth and scattered to the floor.

When the waiter, horrified, ran over, the old man was dead. It needed no medical training to be sure of that: the open eyes, bloodless face, much distorted, and that peculiar meal-sack limpness so familiar to soldiers, all told the same story. Finally, although the waiter didn't notice it, there was the unmistakable odor of bitter almonds, the hallmark of potassium cyanide …

"Suicide is absolutely out of the question," Lieutenant Trask said, atypically dogmatic for a cautious man whose plausible preconceptions had often been shattered by a chancy universe.

Cyriack Skinner Grey, relaxed but attentive, raised his bushy brows at the detective's vehemence, and shifted in the wheelchair. He glanced at the ammeter, assuring himself that the big nickel-silver battery-pack under the seat was being charged via a cord from the wall-socket, and returned his gaze to Trask.

"What makes you so sure?" he asked.

"Because the old guy was getting married on Sunday—to a lovely woman of thirty-four; young enough to be his daughter, in fact. I know," the detective added quickly, "people sometimes panic before a wedding, but Burrington's just not the type—a cheerful, practical, outgoing old fellow. No matter what hit him he'd fight back; that's his track record. Invented a ribbonless typewriter that used a reservoir of ink flowing into hollow keys. Made his first million by the age of twenty-seven. They tried to steal his patent, but he fought like a tiger and won. No, Burrington's not the suicidal type, believe me."

"I'm not sure there is such a thing," Grey said, "but let's accept your argument provisionally." He pressed a button on one arm of the chair, and a ceramic mug of steaming Kona coffee rose from a little well. He handed it to Trask, who smiled his thanks. No matter how often he drank the brew, its non-acrid strength delighted his palate. Nobody else had coffee like that; unique. "If not suicide, then either accident or murder—which do you suggest?"

"I'd have to say murder. Accident is nearly impossible. You don't find much cyanide around a restaurant. In fact nobody uses the stuff at all, barring, maybe, photographers. Even exterminators work entirely with gas, and the coroner found potassium cyanide in Burrington's stomach."

"I agree that accident is most unlikely," Grey admitted. "But you did say only the waiter came near him that night."

"True," was the rueful reply. "And that's why I'm here. To pick your brains again and find out, if I can, how the old man was poisoned when nobody approached him. I have to clear the waiter; not only no possible motive, but he's worked there over fifteen years, always served Burrington, and loved—I don't exaggerate—him. They just hit it off from the start."

"If murder, what was the motive? And whose?"

"Ah," the detective said. "An excellent question, and plenty of answers. Burrington has three no-good relatives—two nephews and a niece. They're the children of his only sister, who died ten years ago. She was not much herself, I've learned; just the opposite kind from her brother. A sour, nit-picking, stingy, silly woman, who spoiled the three kids. Oh, Burrington helped, I guess; handed out the goodies too lavishly, but you expect that from a rich uncle—a bachelor to boot.

"Anyhow," Trask continued, finishing the coffee and handing Grey the empty mug, "they have an obvious motive. Here's their uncle, worth all that dough, with them his only heirs, and now he's marrying a woman who could get everything and outlive the lot of 'em besides."

The scientist refilled the mug and passed it to Trask, who grinned, pleased that the little ploy had worked so well. He hated to ask for more, since it was bad enough to expect free help—sure, the city was always short of money, but Grey deserved a fee—without cadging refreshments.

"But surely," Grey said, "he's not cutting them out altogether."

"No. I talked to his lawyer. Burrington planned to leave them something, but, you see, they'd already had—and misused—quite a lot of his money, so most of it was meant for Susan Lake—that's the woman he intended to marry. It's a matter of the difference between a hundred thousand each and three million—and if that's not enough motive for a murder, then I never handled a bar-killing over the price of a drink!"

"What do you know about the nephews and niece? Are they capable of such a cold-blooded act?"

"To answer the last part first, I have to say, cynical as it may seem, who isn't when there's so much money involved? But as to the three suspects, they are George, Quentin, and Melissa—all Burringtons, naturally—or half so, by blood; actually, they're children of a man named Talbot, who married Burrington's sister. Well, George runs a travel agency—set up for him years ago by his indulgent uncle. I should say that Talbot never amounted to much, and did nothing for his kids. It was Uncle Hector to the rescue all the time. Which is why," he added, uncharacteristically bitter, "I hate this particular killing. Here's a nice old guy who knocked himself out for the three, and one of them sure as hell murdered him!"

"Hi, Lieutenant! What'd you lose this time—the official helicopter?"

The query came from Edgar Grey, who had just bounded into the room. He seldom moved at less than a gallop, being blessed with abundant energy and a healthy, fourteen-year-old body. His brain was a kind of illegal alien in its skull, belonging more properly in that of a future Galois. He now gave his father a broad wink. "Can you find a lost helicopter, Dad?"

"Nothing is lost this time," the scientist said rather gravely. "We're talking about a particularly heartless murder."

"I'm sorry," the boy said. "I didn't know ..."

"Of course not," Trask said. "No harm done. I was getting too involved anyhow. Well, as I was saying, George has this agency, but he's lousy at business. Rarely makes a living, and will buy anything on credit he can con people into selling.

"Then there's Quentin. He claims to be an artist, and has a gallery, too. Needless to say, the only person ever known to have bought one of his alleged paintings is—you guessed it—Uncle Hector. Who also subsidizes the gallery. Both men, I might add, are married, Quentin for

128

the third time, and their wives are not very frugal or good home-makers either.

"Finally, we have Melissa. The name, I'm told, means 'honey' or the like, but she's a sharp-tongued spinster, as I can testify after talking to her; more like vinegar. She teaches drama at Wentworth College—that's a small private one; probably you know it. Oh, for what it's worth, George's thirty-two, Quentin, twenty-nine, and Melissa thirty-six. Many years ahead of them, presumably, and money greatly needed."

Trask gulped the last of his coffee, and started to hand the mug to Grey, but Edgar did that for him, no doubt to demonstrate his new seriousness.

"An excellent summary," Grey said. "It would seem," he added slowly, "that if one of the three is guilty, he or she must have been in the restaurant that night. Is that the case?"

"Wish I knew," the detective said. "I've grilled everybody the manager and help can identify as being there at the time, but that still leaves at least six or eight customers they didn't know."

"Surely they'd remember the nephews and niece—or hadn't any of the three ever gone there?"

"That's right; they never had. Burrington liked to eat alone. Came in every Thursday, as I've said, and precisely at seven. Always took the same table, too, against the south wall."

"So they may have known, even without eating there, about his regularity."

"Good point; I've given it a lot of thought. Whoever killed him almost certainly planned it all in terms of Burrington's routine. Easy enough for one of the three to go there any other night and inspect the layout. For that matter, it's possible the killer looked through the window some Thursday to spot the old man's table and eating habits."

"Which they must have learned from him, inevitably by now," Grey pointed out. "He's been going there for—how long?—over twenty years you said, I believe."

"Right."

"Anything I can do?" Edgar asked, rather wistfully.

129

"We may need your help later," Trask said, being tactful. This did not appear to be a leg job; more one for Grey's plausible inferences.

"I don't suppose you were able to seal off the Tudor Room," the scientist said. "That would be hard on the hotel, and perhaps unjustified."

"Oddly enough—and maybe it's lucky, judging from your question—we were. You see, they were closing down anyhow; time for their vacation, plus some remodeling. So to date, nothing's been touched. Why did you ask—got any ideas?"

"Nary a one. But if the poison got into Burrington's food and nobody but the waiter came near him—well, that raises some very intriguing possibilities." He pressed a stud, got a tiny flask of brandy from a recess, and took a sip. "Sorry," he said. "Forgot." He jabbed something else; a Havana cigar rolled into his hand; deftly he tossed it to Trask. A buzzer sounded, and the detective started.

"Battery charge completed," Grey said, smiling. He pulled the plug. "What I'd like from you now is all the data on who was in the restaurant at the critical time."

"Got all the information here," the detective said, picking up his briefcase. "I'll leave it with you and hope something develops. As it is, I'm almost certain one of the three killed Burrington, but I don't know who or how." He looked at Edgar, expecting a jibe, but the boy was more perceptive than Trask realized; he had been carefully reared, and had his father for an example.

"I'm sure Dad will be able to help," was all Edgar said. "And good luck, Lieutenant."

After he had studied Trask's well-drawn sketch of the restaurant, showing the exact location of each table, Grey read the testimony given by known patrons. It was their impressions of the few strangers in the Tudor Room that most interested him, for the germ of an idea was developing in his mind. One thing he had in common with all first-rate scientists was a highly active imagination. It is a great mistake to think of science as a cut-and-dried "method"—imagination is always paramount; the lab-work is only to test hypotheses.

Two hours went by; then Grey put the folders aside, slid deeper into his chair, and activated the theater of his brain. He saw the dimly lit room; Burrington eating, occasionally turning to acknowledge a friendly wave from some acquaintance a few tables away. Grey's inner eye shifted to the people nearest to the victim. Distance was clearly a vital factor if his hypothesis had any merit. A couple at one table; he was tall and thin; she small and round. He thought of them as the Jack Sprats ... neither could be one of the Unholy Three—as he tagged Burrington's nephews and niece ... so that left one table ... flamboyant old lady; almost a Phyllis Diller act ... fluff, feathers, bright colors ... but also much too old ... sixtyish ... you can hire a killer, he reminded himself; needn't be do-it-yourself murder ... somebody in the kitchen ... but Trask had checked that out; not very likely; no strangers in there while the Burrington dinner was being made and served ...

Sighing, he sat up again, touched a little lever, and received a small apple, glossy-green in color, with the crisp tartness he liked. He ate it slowly, his imagination still active. Suddenly he stiffened, reactivating the theater ... little fires glowed in his deep-set eyes ... it could be—it could just be! ... a job for Edgar—some of his legwork— might put some meat on the bare bones of his theory ...

Two days later Grey phoned Trask. "I suppose you tested the food for cyanide," he said.

"Of course, but we didn't find any."

"Some of the peas were spilled when Burrington collapsed, I believe."

"That's so. What about it?"

"Did you get all those on the floor?"

There was a puzzled silence.

"I doubt it; my God, you know how green peas can roll! The ones in the bowl had no poison, so that should settle the point."

"Not all of them are equal rollers," Grey said dryly. "Some are more equal than others." Before the lieutenant could reply he added, "Colonel Stoopnagel—before your time—had a joke about something that looked like an umbrella but wasn't for when it looked like rain but didn't. I'm thinking of something that looks like a green pea but isn't—suppose you go over that floor with a good three-cell flashlight, pinching everything that resembles a pea."

"I'll do it," Trask said hollowly. "But if anybody else ever made such a suggestion—"

"It's not likely to happen again," Grey assured him, his mouth twitching briefly.

An hour later he got the return call.

"Five of them!" the detective exulted. "So help me—five little, green balls—cyanide, sure as hell. How did you know—but even more—how did they get them into his dish?"

"No 'them'—it took only one. The others were misses. Why not come over, and I'll explain."

When Trask arrived half an hour later, Grey turned to Edgar. "Tell him what you learned at Wentworth College."

"Well," the boy said, "Melissa Talbot not only teaches drama, she coaches the college Players. What's more," he added meaningly, "I found out she acts in their shows—and she's good as old ladies; she was Miss Prism in 'The Importance of Being Earnest' last year."

"I know you're leading up to something," Trask said, "but frankly you lost me at the last fork."

"You remember the flashy old woman near Burrington," the scientist said.

"Of course."

"Miss Melissa Talbot, made up for the part. Naturally, nobody knew her; the help had never met her, and even Hector didn't recognize her in that wild costume."

"But she never went near him!" Trask objected.

"Didn't have to—and wouldn't dare, obviously. That would have made her a prime suspect. You may also recall she had one of those long, Phyllis Diller type cigarette holders. Only, like the peas, it wasn't. Actually, it was—"

"Br-r-rother!" the detective exclaimed. "A blowgun!"

"Close enough. I think of it more as an old fashioned beanblower we had as kids; that's what triggered my theory—a mighty wild one it seemed at first. But in the badly-lit room she could put the thing in and out of her mouth—as nervous people or those trying to quit smoking often do—and take as many shots as needed. Who would notice? You got Edgar in for my light-meter check; those little electric table-candles leave even a seated person in a kind of penumbra from the shoulders up. To steal the old Mark Twain joke, you have to strike a match to see if the light is on! Anyhow, she finally made a bull's-eye on Burrington's dish of peas. She must have missed at least five times—the ones you found on the floor. Not surprising; no easy shot even from only twelve feet away, as I scaled it on your sketch-map. Some were bound to hit the table and roll off, being more lively, I'd guess, than the soft, real ones. Probably, too, she shot only when he turned his head to greet somebody."

"How come she didn't poison herself? You can't hold cyanide in your mouth like beans—it dissolves fast, and curtains!"

"She wouldn't do it that way. For each try she could put a pill down the tube, then puff through narrowed lips at the mouth end. It's easy enough; Edgar and I checked it—but only with beans, not poison!"

"But where'd she get the cyanide? As I said, it's not found in many places. Some pharmacies have it, I think, but wouldn't dare sell any except to some qualified official or technician."

"That's something else I discovered," Edgar said with pride in his voice. "By the way, I posed as a high-school student planning to enroll at Wentworth, and got a kind of V.I.P. Tour, since they'd heard of Dad. Not that I meant it—it's M.I.T. or Cal Tech for me."

"Naturally," Trask said blandly. "You could gulp down the curriculum at Wentworth over a weekend—and still have time to chase butterflies. But what else did you find out?"

"I talked to lots of the kids in all departments, getting in idle questions about Melissa when feasible. I soon learned she'd been going into the chem lab, which she'd never done before. Plenty of KCN on the shelves in there; I saw it."

"So with a pinch of the poison, and some dye, she could make phony peas by the dozen, right?" Then he gulped in dismay. "It's a lovely theory, and I'd bet my life on it, but there's no way in the world to make a solid case. By now the trick holder's gone; the costume's burned or buried; and the cyanide washed down the sink. She's home free—unless her nerve cracks. Which isn't likely," he added wryly. "Anybody with the guts to pull a job that bold …"

"I can't help you there," Grey said quietly. "But maybe you'll think of something."

"I'll give it a damned good try," Trask said in a grim voice. "He was a real nice old guy."

Three days later Grey blinked in surprise on reading the headline in his morning paper:

HUNGRY TRANSIENT SEES BIZARRE KILLING!
COULD CRACK BURRINGTON CASE!

Tom Bentley, an unemployed carpenter from Missouri, has told the police of looking through the window of the Hotel Empire's Tudor Room and seeing a woman shooting pellets of some kind through a 'sort of funny cigarette holder.' If Bentley can identify the mysterious old lady, the revolting poison murder of Hector MacNeil Burrington, which has baffled the police, may soon be cleared up …

Grey's eyebrows rose, and a tiny choking sound left his lips.
That evening Trask phoned him. "You saw the paper, I suppose."
"I did," Grey said. "A surprise witness; how very handy!"
"I knew you'd see through it. But she didn't." He paused, then said in a tense voice: "She hanged herself this afternoon." Another pause. "Not what I had in mind. I hoped she'd run, or talk too much … you see, I had no case; she was too damned thorough. We checked her table for prints, but drew a blank. Our main hope was the silverware and glasses, but they were in the dishwasher long before we suspected her. Besides, she was careful; had only a salad, and just toyed with that. Bet she didn't touch a thing but the fork, and then wiped that clean. So we couldn't place her on the scene at all. Then I thought maybe she'd left a print on the restaurant bill, but no; unlike

most people, who pick it up automatically to check the arithmetic or figure the tip, she just left money on top of it in the dish."

"I wonder if the other two had a hand in it—the planning, if not the execution."

"We'll never know," Trask said sourly. "They'll collect their four or five million each, and ride the Gravy Train into the sunset. And I assure you from long experience, no thunderbolt will strike from the heavens, either." His voice softened. "And yet to see that wretched, greedy woman hanging there … I don't feel even one-third victorious."

"I know," Grey said. "And I sympathize. I agree with Donne that any man's death—or woman's—diminishes me. But none of this tragic affair is your fault, and Burrington seems to have been a fine old man. He was not flawed like King Lear, and didn't deserve a Goneril-Niece."

They left it at that.

The Scientist and the Heavenly Alibi

"What can even a damn good D.A. like Pete Loret do," Lt. Trask asked almost plaintively, "when the killer has a solid alibi from God— or, if you prefer, Copernicus?"

The question sounded rather rhetorical, but the detective was implying the answer—consult, through me, Cyriack Skinner Grey, the man in the wheelchair, placed there many years earlier by a mountaineering accident. A distinguished scientist, his reduced mobility had forced him to give up the active field-work he loved in favor of a more sedentary career as criminologist, to which he brought all his laboratory expertise and wide-ranging theoretical knowledge of biology, physics, and chemistry. Above all, he specialized in practical, applied logic—plausible inferences, he called it.

Now his deep-socketed eyes, black as coal, twinkled as he quipped: "Copernicus definitely existed, but as to your first alibi-maker, good ontological evidence is lacking." He was a skeptic by temperament, of whom it was once reported—the story was undoubtedly apocryphal, having been told before about others—that while driving to a seminar with a colleague, they had seen a flock of sheep on a farm near the highway.

"They've just been sheared, I'd say," his friend remarked.

Grey took a long look, thought a moment, and replied, "On this side, anyhow."

Trask may have been recalling this, since he badly needed a tough-minded approach to his situation.

"My problem is that I know the guy committed a premeditated, cold-blooded murder, but unless he made the sun stand still, was two hundred miles away, here in town, when it happened. There are no bullet trains, we've ruled out any kind of plane, so it had to be by road, and traffic is pretty heavy. Nobody could cover that distance in only an hour unless it was all done at Indianapolis, so—"

"Sun stand still," Grey said, cocking his head. "His name isn't Joshua, I presume. Tell me about it."

"Sure; that's why I'm here. This fellow, William Davis Parker, is half owner of a valuable cattle ranch two hundred miles from town. It's mainly the land, near Salinas, that's worth dough; five million is mentioned. Well, Parker seems to be a gambler and wastrel, and he owes a hell of a lot of money to people who employ ex-wrestlers or whatever with very bad manners. So to raise some cash in a hurry and save all 200+ of his bones from being broken, Parker sets up a meet with his partner, Tom Everett, at some isolated part of the ranch. There he kills him dead. Nothing fancy; no pistol that might be traced, but just a hunk of rock. One or two good blows to the left temple. Then he drives back to town. Nobody has seen him or can put him at the scene of the crime. And, in fact, he has a photo, a clear color slide taken by a top 35 mm camera by his wife, showing him on the walk in front of a store only about an hour after the crime was committed."

He paused for breath and to collect his thoughts. Grey pressed a button on the arm of his state-of-the-art chair, which he designed, and drew a small cup of black Kona coffee, which Trask accepted with a nod of thanks.

"The thing is," he continued, "it's obvious from the sunlight falling on the west side of the north-south street that it's no later than ten a.m., only about an hour after the murder, according to the coroner, although we also know from the two ranch-hands who found the body. And, as I've said, there's no way Parker could have driven two hundred miles that fast. He spends more time in town, handling ranch taxes and such."

Grey frowned. "What about the day?" he asked. "Couldn't he have taken the picture the day before, or even after? I assume you didn't arrest him—if you did—right after the murder."

"Good point," the detective said. "One of the first things we thought of." Then he added, with seeming irrelevance, "Do you know that fine old 1948 movie, 'Call Northside 777'?"

The scientist reflected briefly, then replied, "Wasn't that the one where the reporter cleared an innocent man of a murder charge? Jimmy Stewart was the reporter, I believe."

"Right. And he did it," Trask said with emphasis, "by establishing a critical date, which he got by blowing up a photo of a newspaper on a rack until the date could be read. Which is," he added, "exactly what our lab did in this case. And, unfortunately, Parker was on the walk, a few feet from the rack, when the photo was taken. And it wasn't doctored; we made sure of that. If the negative had been reversed, say, on a print, the writing would be reversed on the newspaper; but even that's academic, since we have the original slide, and it checks out."

"I see what you mean," Grey said thoughtfully, his eyes shining. "An alibi from the heavens, from astronomy, so to speak." It was clearly an unusual case, the sort that delighted him especially, because a point of science was the crux.

"I can imagine faking sunlight over a small area, say with photoflood lamps, but you'd need several the size of buses to light up a street."

"That's right. Oddly, there was a case years ago where floodlights were set up outside a picture window to make the room inside look as it would by day. That alibi didn't hold up; I think some smart cop spotted an impossible sundial shadow." He peered at his watch. "Wow, I gotta go," he said, gulping the last of the coffee. "I'll leave you the documents and photos, then it'll be up to you, Copernicus— and Joshua!" And grinning, he left.

When Trask had gone, Grey drew a little glass of peach brandy from a spigot on the wheelchair, and as he sipped it, read the reports slowly and with deep concentration, after which, using a Coddington lens, he studied both the slide and some prints made from it. Then he activated what he thought of as his Theater of the Mind, giving a splendid imagination full play to roam over all plausible inferences concerning the fascinating puzzle left to him.

Light—a matter of light—sunlight … he thought of the long, bitter controversy about its true nature—particles or waves? … a battle of titans: Newton, Huygens, Maxwell … and the answer, paradoxically, ambiguous; light could be, and often was, both at once …

He studied the slide again, noting for the first time a small pothole in the street. It was full of water, and, at the bottom, some broken glass, a few twigs, and other debris. Good lens, obviously. He could see the bits clearly. Suddenly he stiffened in the chair. Clearly? Too clearly! What was the inference? There could be only one. Wheeling rapidly to the phone, he called Trask …

While waiting for the desk sergeant to run down his busy superior, Grey flipped the switch on his built-in radio, getting, as always, the classical music station, KLEF. By a wild coincidence that delighted him, he came in on the first movement of Haydn's "Sunrise Quartet." Maybe Jung had a point with his synchronicity theories, he thought, smiling.

When Trask came on the phone, Grey told him, briskly cheerful, "Come see me—I may just have Copernicus on the ropes." As a sometime champion welterweight boxer in college, the analogy came naturally to him, however inappropriate in this case—fancy the great Polish astronomer in the ring! "But," he went on, "I need one more piece of information, a vital one. Find out, if you don't already know—the photo doesn't show it—what building is on the east side of the street … Fine; clear that up, and drop by."

Later, he was saying to the detective, "It was the pothole full of water that gave it away. You see—there's not only no glare you'd expect from direct sunlight, but visibility is good even to the bottom of the water. What does that suggest to you? What gives that kind of vision?"

Puzzled, Trask frowned; then his face brightened, and he said, "Polaroid glasses! I've used them occasionally while fishing. But—" he was still confused—"if Parker wore them, that wouldn't change the photo …"

"Of course not," Grey said, smiling. "But light is polarized quite a bit by any sizeable piece of plate glass. So when you told me about the big warehouse across the street with all those windows, it clinched the case. Parker posed for the picture not at 10 in the morning, but nearer 3 p.m. The western sun was reflected massively by the warehouse window, seeming to shine on the west side of the street as in the morning. At this time of the year, a sunny afternoon is almost certain, and who would see his wife snap, unobtrusively, with a small 35 mm camera, a picture of her husband on the walk by—deliberately, I'm sure—a rack of newspapers? Very likely he also made sure by a few days' observations that some papers were still there in the afternoon—or the rack refilled, perhaps. Does all this make your case for the D.A.?"

"You just bet it does," Trask exulted. "All the other evidence is overwhelming. We needed only to break the alibi and prove he could have come back to town much later. The very fact of his setting up a phony photo is the last nail in Parker's coffin. Why would an innocent man fake the picture?"

"Give me some time," Grey said gravely, but his eyes shone with humor, "and I may come up with a plausible inference to explain that."

"Please don't!" Trask exclaimed, smiling. "I'm out of here before you do just that and make me doubt my case."

The Scientist and the One-Word Clue

Cyriack Skinner Grey sat up in his gadget-ridden, elaborate wheelchair, studied the large, glossy photographic print, and frowned.

"I see what you mean," he said. "Somebody really tore the place apart. What was he—or they—after?"

"Wallace's notes, almost certainly. He's a top investigative reporter who was probably closing in on corruption at the state capitol—so they had to kill him, and did. Those notes would have made the D.A.'s case, but now Brandon will have a very tough time making serious charges stick. He just doesn't have enough."

Grey's guest, more accurately, client, Lieutenant of Detectives Trask was clearly downcast.

"What a mess," Grey said. "Pity. He had some nice things. Prints, books, sculptures, all in good taste. And that was a top-of-the-line hi-fi set-up they trashed. Now mostly junk."

"Not just a search," Trask said. "Some vindictiveness, too. The big-shots must have really hated Wallace. No need to go on such a rampage after they stabbed the poor guy to death."

"No clues?" Grey asked.

"Only one," Trask said glumly. "And it's driving me nuts—which is why I'm here."

He looked so downcast that Grey, whose wheelchair was fearfully and wonderfully made, thanks to his imagination and engineering background, pressed a stud in one arm, producing from a tiny faucet a trickle of coffee, which he caught in a small cup and offered to the detective. It was black, strong enough to float a lead sinker, and almost hot enough to melt it. Trask took it gratefully, brightening as he sipped the potent brew. It was Grey's own favorite Kona.

"I know there's almost nothing to go on," the detective said, "but maybe you can come up with something. You almost always do," he added hopefully.

He had reasonable grounds for optimism. Grey, a widower and research scientist of genius, had been immobilized permanently many years ago in a climbing accident. Unable to function exactly as before, he had become a crime consultant, making good use of his expertise in biology, physics, and chemistry. He specialized, however, mainly in what he called plausible inferences, meaning more emphasis on logic and imagination than technical competence, of which he had plenty when it was needed.

"Well," he said now, "what about your one clue."

"As I said," Trask told him, "after they stabbed Wallace—they wouldn't risk a noisy shot, probably; needed quiet time to search— they thought he was done for. But when they left, with or without the notes, he lived just long enough to scribble one word on the fly-leaf of a book they'd tossed on the floor near him. The word was 'Thais,' " he added ruefully. "What's the point, I wonder, of being so damned general? Sure, there are a lot of Orientals in the neighborhood, refugees, mostly, and some, I suppose from Thailand, but that's hardly a real lead. Besides, how or why would they be involved with state political hanky-panky; that's out of character."

"I agree," Grey said. "Surely, if he had a name, it would be that of a key figure in the corruption, not a nationality, far too vague and general. Well," he went on, "leave me all the data, the photos and dossiers, and I'll give it my best shot."

"Right," Trask said. "You're my only chance. 'Thais'!" he said indignantly. "Big help!"

Alone, Grey tapped another faucet, drawing himself an ounce of apricot brandy. He pressed another button and the local all-classics radio station, KLEF, came on very softly, but with excellent tone. Then he opened what he thought of as his Theater of the Mind—a brainstorming visualization of possibilities, probabilities, and the plausible inferences they suggested.

He read all the reports and background papers; he scrutinized, using a magnifying glass, the excellent photos of the murder scene; and gave the Theater full play. But nothing of value resulted. One cryptic, fuzzy word was not enough.

The scientist sighed, lay back in the wheelchair, and let the music envelop him. It was his policy, well known to researchers, to back off and let the subconscious take over.

Violent death, Grey thought. Investigative reporter, closing in on corrupt politics, makes notes, so they kill him to save their skins. Hired guns, no doubt … only one clue … death … music, musical death …

Suddenly he stiffened in his chair, his dark eyes growing bright. That music, so sad, voluptuous—lovely; he knew it well, and so—of course!—did Wallace, what with all that hi-fi equipment, and the reference books on symphonies, operas, instruments …

"By God!" Grey exclaimed softly; and taking the cellular phone from its recess, he called Trask.

That call was returned three hours later.

"We found the notes!" Trask said exultantly. "An audio cassette labeled 'Highlights from Thaïs.' Wallace had recorded all his key data over the music—and the killers missed it. Can't blame them; just another pre-recorded cassette among dozens. Now," he added grimly, "we have names, dates, all the hard evidence Brandon will need. You really pulled off a miracle—not for the first time."

"It was the music on KLEF that steered me right," the scientist said. "When it dawned on me that I was hearing 'The Death of Thaïs,' a very moving, gorgeous climax—Beverly Sills, by the way—I realized that Wallace was not writing 'Thais,' the Asians, but 'Thaïs,' Massenet's splendid opera. What a pity," he added softly, "that he wasn't able, or didn't remember to add, that dieresis—two little dots—over the 'i'. That would have tipped us immediately."

Trask smiled. "Speak for yourself—I'm more a jazz fan. I wouldn't know 'Thaïs' from 'The Flying Dutchman'!"

Checklist of Sources

The checklist below gives the original publication source for each of the stories included in this collection:

"The Scientist and the Bagful of Water," first published in *Ellery Queen's Mystery Magazine*, November 1965.

"The Scientist and the Wife Killer," first published in *Ellery Queen's Mystery Magazine*, January 1966.

"The Scientist and the Vanished Weapon," first published in *Ellery Queen's Mystery Magazine*, March 1966.

"The Scientist and the Obscene Crime," first published in *Ellery Queen's Mystery Magazine*, September 1966.

"The Scientist and the Multiple Murder," first published in *Ellery Queen's Mystery Magazine*, February 1967.

"The Scientist and the Invisible Safe," first published in *Ellery Queen's Mystery Magazine*, May 1967.

"The Scientist and the Two Thieves," first published in *Alfred Hitchcock's Mystery Magazine*, June 1974.

"The Scientist and the Time Bomb," first published in *Alfred Hitchcock's Mystery Magazine*, August 1974.

"The Scientist and the Platinum Chain," first published in *Alfred Hitchcock's Mystery Magazine*, September 1974.

"The Scientist and the Exterminator," first published in *Alfred Hitchcock's Mystery Magazine*, November 1974.

"The Scientist and the Missing Pistol," first published in *Mike Shayne Mystery Magazine*, January 1975.

"The Scientist and the Stolen Rembrandt," first published in *Alfred Hitchcock's Mystery Magazine*, February 1975.

"The Scientist and the Impassable Gulf," first published in *Mike Shayne Mystery Magazine*, October 1975.

"The Scientist and the Poisoner," previously unpublished.

"The Scientist and the Heavenly Alibi," previously unpublished.

"The Scientist and the One-Word Clue," previously published.

About the Author

Arthur Porges was born in Chicago, Illinois on August 20, 1915. One of four brothers, he was educated at Roosevelt High School and Senn High School before enrolling at The Lewis Institute where he achieved a Bachelor of Science Degree in Mathematics. After the successful completion of his postgraduate studies, through which he attained Masters Degrees in Mathematics and Engineering from the Illinois Institute of Technology, Porges enlisted in the U.S. Army in 1942. During the Second World War he served as an artillery instructor, teaching algebra and trigonometry to field personnel. He was stationed at various military installations including Camp White in Oregon, Fort Sill, Oklahoma, Camp Roberts, California and at Barnes Hospital in Vancouver, Washington. After the war Porges returned to Illinois and taught mathematics at the Western Military Academy, going on to serve as an assistant professor at De Paul University. Having taught at Occidental College in Los Angeles for a brief stint in the late forties, Porges made a permanent move to California in 1951 and spent several years as a mathematics teacher at Los Angeles City College. During this period he wrote and sold short stories as a sideline. In 1957, Porges retired from teaching to write full-time. He went on to publish hundreds of short stories in numerous magazines and newspapers. Many of his stories appeared in *Alfred Hitchcock's Mystery Magazine*, *Ellery Queen's Mystery Magazine*, *Amazing Stories* and *The Magazine of Fantasy and Science Fiction*. His fiction spanned several genres, with tales ranging from science fiction and fantasy to horror, mysteries, and so on. At his most prolific his work was appearing in three or four periodicals in one month alone. Among his best known stories are "The Ruum," "The Rats," "No Killer Has Wings," "The Mirror" and "The Rescuer." Seven previous book collections of his short stories have been published: *Three Porges Parodies and a Pastiche* (1988), *The Mirror and Other Strange Reflections* (2002), *Eight Problems in Space: The Ensign De Ruyter Stories* (2008), *The Adventures of Stately Homes and Sherman Horn* (2008), *The Calabash of Coral Island and Other Early Stories* (2008), *The Miracle of the Bread and Other Stories* (2008) and *The Devil and Simon Flagg and Other Fantastic Tales* (2009). Several of his poems were collected in the book *Spring, 1836: Selected Poems* (2008). A keen birdwatcher and an avid reader, Porges wrote many articles, essays and poems, most of which were published in the *Monterey Herald*. After spells in Laguna Beach and San Clemente, Porges moved north, eventually settling in Pacific Grove. He passed away, at the age of 90, in May 2006.

Lightning Source UK Ltd.
Milton Keynes UK
UKHW011027110121
376834UK00001B/250

9 780955 694240